Sugarplums, Spells & Silver Bells

By

Ellen Dugan

Sugarplums, Spells & Silver Bells
Copyright @ Ellen Dugan 2017
Cover art designed by Kyle Hallemeier
Cover image: fotolia: bublik_polina
"Legacy Of Magick" logo designed by Kyle Hallemeier
Copy Editing and Formatting by Libris in CAPS

This is a work of fiction. Names, characters, businesses, organizations, places, events and incidents either are the product of the author's imagination or are used fictitiously. Any resemblance to actual persons, living or dead, events, or locales is entirely coincidental.

No part of this book may be reproduced, or stored in a retrieval system, or transmitted in any other form or by any means electronic, mechanical, photocopying, recording or otherwise without the express written permission of the publisher.

Published by Ellen Dugan

Other titles by Ellen Dugan

THE LEGACY OF MAGICK SERIES

Legacy of Magick, Book 1

Secret of the Rose, Book 2

Message of the Crow, Book 3

Beneath An Ivy Moon, Book 4

Under The Holly Moon, Book 5

The Hidden Legacy, Book 6

Spells Of The Heart, Book 7

Sugarplums, Spells & Silver Bells, Book 8

Magick & Magnolias, Book 9 (Coming 2018)

THE GYPSY CHRONICLES

Gypsy At Heart, Book 1

Gypsy Spirit, Book 2 (Coming 2018)

ACKNOWLEDGMENTS

To my fabulous crew of beta readers: Becca, Erin, Ro and Shawna. Thanks for your speed reading skills, the notes, and of course for patiently listening to me while I plotted my way through this novella. Thanks to Kyle for the enchanting cover and for bringing Violet to life, and to Mitchell for the editing.

This one's for the fans! Happy Holidays and Brightest Blessings!

Christmas waves a magic wand over this world,

And behold, everything is softer and more beautiful.

-Norman Vincent Peale

The Sugarplum Fairy herself could have made no grander gesture.

-Shana Alexander

PROLOGUE

"I don't care what you think," I said to my familiar. "I won't resort to magick to win the holiday decorating contest."

Tank, a gray British shorthair, narrowed his bright yellow feline eyes and made a chirping noise that sounded suspiciously like a chuckle.

I glanced down when he rubbed against my ankles. "This year, Tank," I said, adding the last of the amethyst ornaments to the main display tree. "We are winning a prize for best decorated shop in the William's Ford Holiday Happening."

"Meow?" Tank tipped his head, sat beside me and began to paw at a silver star.

"Our Sugarplum Fairy theme is perfect." I stacked up the empty ornament boxes, carried them to the storage tub, and placed them inside. "When we open the flower shop tomorrow we are going to have our best Black Friday sales, *ever.* You'll see."

I checked the clock and rolled my shoulders. It had been a long day. It was almost 10 p.m. and my mother and I had been in a holiday decorating frenzy since two o'clock in the afternoon. It had been our family tradition for years. Eat an early Thanksgiving dinner, then dive in and flip the shop to holiday décor on our day off. As florists it was vital to our business to have the store decked out to coordinate with the seasons, since this boosted sales and our seasonal arrangement orders.

Thanks to our Sugarplum Fairy theme, I was finally able to celebrate the holiday with my favorite color—purple. Some folks would probably be surprised by the untraditional hue...but it would stand out and make us distinctive. I should know, as it's my signature color. Even my long blonde hair was streaked and dip dyed a soft lavender, and I loved the ombre effect.

Some folks think that I'm quirky, but I prefer

the term *unique*—thank you very much. Whenever anyone rolls their eyes at me I'm quick to point out that my mother started it all with her choice for my first name.

I'm Violet O'Connell. Florist, Witch about town, and purple aficionado.

I'd become full partners with my mother Cora in the flower shop four years ago, and for the past few weeks we'd been slaving away creating garlands, a variety of wreaths, and smaller trimmed holiday trees at my mother's house. This year's theme was a closely guarded secret, and our color scheme was purple, white and silver with pops of teal and pink.

Today, we'd finally hauled everything in and decorated our little hearts out. After my mother had headed home, I was left thinking about a glass of wine and a long hot bath. All I had to do was drag myself upstairs to my own apartment.

I snapped the lid closed on the storage tote and went to make sure the covering on the front window would stay securely in place until we were ready to unveil the store's holiday display. I double-checked the lock on the front door and slowly turned back around for a critical assessment of the overall effect.

It was perfect! A trio of table top sugarplum theme trees in staggered heights, added a faery tale aura to the room. They featured a heavy emphasis on pastel pink and lavender ornaments and were located centrally in the shop. Also, a large white tree dominated our main display window. The eight foot tree was a show stopper. Covered in sparkling silver and deep amethyst glass ornaments the tree was decorated completely around, as it could be viewed from all sides.

Rich white garlands were draped around the walls of the shop as well. Their swags and swoops were highlighted by twinkling purple and white fairy lights and beautiful shimmering ribbon in silver and metallic plum.

On the big round table in the center of the display area, silver toned trays were out and waiting for the cakepops, candies and cookies for tomorrow evening. The rest of the table itself was covered with votive cups of mercury glass and glistening vases filled with arrangements of coordinating silk flowers, peacock feathers and metallic holly. A large silk bird with plum colored feathers was tucked into a large central arrangement, and the effect was festive and extravagant.

I walked over and trailed my fingers along the table. Round glass ornaments in a variety of sizes in silver, frosted white and every shade of purple were arranged or resting in bowls. A trio of sparkly reindeer pranced across the table, and the entire display was guarded by a large wizard nutcracker. He glittered in tones of lilac and gray, and his wizard's hat added the perfect —and magickal—finishing touch.

Baskets and containers of duplicate ornaments that we'd decorated with were stacked strategically around the sales floor, within easy reach for the customers. Poinsettias in white, pink and red, Christmas cactus, and pots of amaryllis, had been added wherever we had an open space. Our decorated holiday wreaths and swags were ready for purchase, as were a variety of Yuletide tchotchkes and accessories. We were filled to the brim and ready for the holiday rush.

"No other shop on Main Street is going to

come close to this," I said, feeling a bit smug. This year the O'Connells are bagging the prize. No witchcraft necessary."

"Meow," Tank added his opinion.

"It's not about the prize money, Tank," I reminded him, making a small adjustment to an arrangement of ornaments. "It's the bragging rights. The other merchants on Main Street love to wave that ribbon for best decorations around, and by the goddess this year it will be ours."

The only thing left to do was to hang the shop's wreath on the inside of the front door. I picked up the large flocked wreath, which chimed as I lifted it. On closer inspection I realized that not only had my mother covered it with silver and shiny lavender ornaments, she had also worked little silver bells into the design as well.

"Hmmm..." I paused. While I wouldn't resort to using witchcraft to win the contest, I could certainly enchant the shop for a little extra prosperity. "Let's do a little spontaneous magick," I said to myself. "It can't hurt to ensure the store's success. *And* it will help impart a little holiday magick and cheer on all who enter."

I placed the heavy wreath on the interior metal hanger, and considered my options. "If I time the magick to start now, and run until the twenty-fourth of December, I could enchant the *entire* holiday shopping season."

Happy with my plan, I straightened the wreath slightly on the door, lifted my hands, and focused my energy. "Sugarplum spells and silver bells that merrily do ring; peace, prosperity and joy, my magick will now bring. Bless all who enter with happiness, light and cheer; If you need some joy and magick in your life, my call you will hear."

I closed my eyes and envisioned my magick swirling clockwise around the store. Faster and faster the energy spun. I continued to hold that spiraling magick in place, and then closed up the spell. "As I will it, so now must it be. This spell's magick ends at midnight on Christmas Eve."

I flung my hands into the air and the magick dispersed up and out into the ether. Satisfied with the casting, I brushed off my hands, clicked off the lights, and prepared to leave.

***

Blissfully unaware of what I'd unleashed, I marched up to my apartment and tumbled into sleep. While that impromptu Sugarplum spell began to manifest in ways even I would have *never* imagined.

CHAPTER ONE

The William's Ford Holiday Happening would officially kick off at noon on Black Friday. Knowing what retail insanity awaited me, I slept in that morning and enjoyed a leisurely breakfast before prepping for the biggest retail day of the year. I kept the television and radio off, wanting to enjoy the peace and quiet while it lasted.

In keeping with our holiday theme, I had decided to dress up this year for our official open house in the shop. My friend Marie Rousseau had come over and worked on my hair and makeup. When she was all done, I barely recognized myself.

Marie was a true artist, and the makeup was elaborate and theatrical. My lips had been painted in a dark mauve. She had exaggerated the arch of my eyebrows and did the eye makeup in shades of silver, deep plums and pink. The false eyelashes she'd glued on felt a little weird, however they made my blue eyes appear enormous. Miniature rhinestones sparkled above my cheekbones, and Marie teased my hair for height at the top and braided one side away from my face.

"It's sort of Viking princess meets gothic Sugarplum Fairy," I decided, studying my reflection.

Delighted by the results, I zipped up some flat-heeled boots over my black leggings and cinched the ebony lace top around my waist. The top had mulberry trim, flowing lace sleeves, and was perfect for my costume. I grabbed my sheer fairy wings, slid the elastic straps over my shoulders, and left Tank snoozing away in middle of the sofa.

Once I slipped in the back door of the shop I did a final check in the bathroom mirror, pulled the wings higher, and strolled out onto the sales floor.

My mother glanced up from where she was

putting out some sugar cookies for the afternoon shoppers and started to grin. "Violet, that's wonderful!"

"Marie outdid herself."

"I'm going to want pictures," my mother warned me, reaching for her cell phone.

"You always want pictures." I rolled my eyes and studied the customers that were crammed into the shop. A preschool aged little girl was whining and tugging at her mother's hand. The child looked about thirty seconds away from a full blown melt down, but when she spotted me, she gasped and froze.

"Mama." The child's voice was reverent. "It's a fairy."

My mother and I exchanged a knowing look, and she passed me a cookie. I walked over to the child and knelt down to her level. "Hi, I'm Violet," I said, handing her a cookie. "What's your name?"

Tantrum forgotten, the little girl was gobbling her cookie and grinning from ear to ear a moment later.

"Would you mind if I took a picture of you with my daughter?" the young mother asked.

"Sure." I put my arm around the little girl who was dancing in place, and smiled for the camera.

Word went out on Main Street. Within an hour we had children and their parents in a line outside the door, waiting to come in and meet the 'Sugarplum Fairy'. We were so busy that mom called my brothers and step-dad in to help with crowd control. Kevin, who was home on break from college, ran the register. Mom took orders, and wrapped up poinsettias and flowers, and teenage Eddie kept replenishing poinsettias, or wreaths from the back, or bagging purchases whenever necessary.

My step-father Karl, a retired fire-fighter, cheerfully worked crowd control and kept the head count inside from exceeding our maximum limit.

A little before dinner time the crowd had begun to dwindle, and we took advantage of the lull. Karl and Mom refreshed displays and put out more poinsettias. Kevin and Eddie placed the luminaries out front on the sidewalk and lit them. My friend Candice dropped off the cakepops and cookies we'd special ordered from her bakery, and I gave Marie a call, asking her to give me a touch up.

"I think the makeup got worn off from the hugs of all the little kids," I said, sitting in Mom's office with a towel over my blouse.

"I hear you've been quite the sensation on Main Street today," Marie said.

"It's been fun." My eyes were closed as she reattached one of the eyelashes that was coming loose. "The makeup and hair are amazing."

Marie started to reset the makeup with an iridescent powder and a fluffy brush. "You should know, Spirit says: changes are coming to your world."

I shut my eyes against the powder. "Tell Spirit that I don't have time for that during the holiday season."

"You're not going to have a choice, honey." Marie patted my shoulder, signaling that she was finished.

I batted my eyes a few times, testing the eyelashes. "I'll keep that in mind."

"Violet." Marie's voice was low and amused. "Don't say I didn't warn you." With a wink she left.

I didn't have much time to wonder or worry over her cryptic words. Night had fallen, and the Christmas lights on Main Street blinked to life. The judges would be out on the first night of the festivities, and a whole new batch of shoppers and Holiday Happening attendees had arrived to enjoy the lights, the decorations, and to see all the luminaries up and down the street.

The rest of the evening passed in a whirl and rush. The judges came in to review the store's decorations, and I noted some fairly impressed reactions from them. Finally my brothers headed home, and Mom and Karl began to gather up their things.

My mother stood, wringing her hands behind the counter. "Do you think the judges really liked it?"

"Cora, relax," my step-father said, holding out her coat for her. "The store is beautiful."

"I'm telling you," I said, rearranging the last of the sweets on the main table, "we've got this contest in the bag. When Kevin ran a report an hour ago he said we'd broken our sales records."

"Are you sure you're alright to stay and close

up alone?" she asked.

"Mom, it's almost nine o'clock. The crowd has thinned out." It took fifteen more minutes, but I managed to shoo Mom and Karl out the back door. I locked it behind them and enjoyed the quiet for the first time in several hours.

I worked my way up front, straightening as I went. Finally I made it to the front door, opened it and checked up and down Main Street. Sure enough we were down to the last of the die hard shoppers. I took a deep breath, enjoying the crisp, cold air. As I flipped the sign over to 'Closed', I caught movement out of the corner of my eye.

A child stood staring into our shop's front window. Alone.

I swung my gaze around. There was no one else close by. "Sweetie, where are your parents?" I asked.

The child turned and smiled. I could see blonde hair tufting out from under a striped knit cap. "I wanted to see the Sugarplum Fairy," the child said. "I've been looking for you for a long time."

"Well, here I am," I said. "Why don't you

come inside and out of the cold." I held out my hand and chilled little fingers clasped mine. *Get her out of the cold, first,* I thought. *Figure out who she is, and then call the police...*

I let the door shut behind us, and the child went directly to the table that held the sweets. "Are these sugarplums?" she asked through chattering teeth and grabbed one of the remaining cakepops from the tray.

"Of course." I touched the girl's face and found it icy. "Let's get you warmed up." I picked her up, set her on the tall work station and grabbed my mother's thick cardigan from her chair. I wrapped the child up in it.

She bit into a cakepop and made a happy sound. "I told my daddy that you were real." Her voice sounded a little smug, and even though she shivered, my first impression of a poor, frightened, lost child shifted.

"What's your name, honey?" I asked.

"Charlotte," she said over a mouthful of cakepop. "Charlotte Leigh."

"Okay, Charlie," I said.

She giggled over that. "Nobody calls me Charlie."

"Well, the Sugarplum Fairy does as she pleases." I winked at her. "Where's your mom and dad? I bet they're pretty worried about you." I glanced towards the window in case a desperate parent was running past. But there was no one.

"My daddy wandered off," Charlie said, matter-of-factly. "He does that sometimes."

My stomach clutched in sympathy. "Would you like some water to drink?" I asked her while the music in the store cued up to Tchaikovsky's "Dance of the Sugarplum Fairy".

"Sure." Charlie began to swing her feet back and forth in time to the music. "I like this song," she announced.

I got a bottle of water out of the mini fridge, twisted off the top and handed it to her. She was very well dressed. That was a high end brand of winter coat she was wearing. She had on heavy jeans, and chamois colored boots. Probably leather.

"How old are you, Charlie?"

She wiped her mouth on the back of her coat sleeve. "Aren't you s'posed to know stuff like that? Santa Claus would know."

Clever little hooligan, I thought. She appeared to be Kindergarten age, possibly first grade. *That made her six maybe?* "Well I was double checking my records." I got another cake pop and held it just out of reach. "So, the Sugarplum fairy thinks you're six years old."

Her eyes lit up. "I'll be six pretty soon!" She reached out and snatched the cakepop so quickly that I could only be impressed. She demolished that too.

"Tell you what Charlie," I said, easing back for the store phone. I'm going to call a friend of mine and see if she can help find your Daddy."

"Can I have another sugarplum?"

"You bet." I grabbed the last two purple sprinkled cakepops and handed them to her. I dialed the police station and waited for the operator to pick up. I explained to the operator how I had found the girl. I relayed what I knew about her: name, age, and how she was dressed.

"Can I get down?" Charlie wanted to know.

I tucked the phone under my ear and helped her down off the high countertop. "Stay inside, okay?" I said.

"I will." She grinned and flashed a missing

front tooth. "It's pretty in here."

"She doesn't seem afraid," I said. "I'm betting she wandered off from her parents." The operator told me she had a unit responding and chuckled hearing Charlie's bright chatter in the background.

"I'll let Officer Bishop know the child is safe and entertained," she said. "Try and keep the child inside until the officer arrives."

"I'll watch for Lexie." I thanked the operator and hung up. Lexie Proctor-Bishop was a friend, and the mother of two young children. She was also a fellow Witch. I felt better knowing Lexie would be the one to help the girl find her parents.

"Purple and pink Christmas trees!" Charlie sounded slightly shocked as she stood in front of the sugarplum candy trees. "I've never seen pink and purple trees before." Suddenly, she spotted the flowers. "You have flowers inside!" She raced to the glass fronted cooler. "Flowers in the winter time." She pressed her face against the glass. "You must be magick."

"Truer words..." I chuckled and found myself thoroughly entertained by my surprise guest.

A few moments later a police car zipped up in front of the shop, red and blue lights flashing. While Charlie chattered on, counting the poinsettias on the sales floor, Lexie climbed out of her cruiser, and a silver haired man jumped out of the back seat.

The father. I realized. He was rushing into the shop ahead of Lexie. "Charlotte!" He called. Despite his distress, the man's face was striking, and somehow...familiar.

Charlie saw him and ran straight for me instead of her father. "Hey!" I laughed as she grabbed ahold and hung on tight. "Charlie, it's going to be okay. He's not mad."

"Charlotte Leigh!" The father's voice was sharp and angry. "I've never been so frightened in my entire life! I've been everywhere—"

"Hey, ratchet that down," I said, wrapping an arm around the girl's shoulders.

The father's lecture stopped mid-sentence. He scowled when our eyes met.

"Easy, Dad." Lexie Proctor-Bishop smoothly stepped forward. "Let me handle this," she said and knelt down at Charlie's level. "Charlotte, My name is Lexie."

Charlie peeped around my leg. "Hi," she said softly. "Are you a police lady?" She reached out and touched the collar of Lexie's uniform.

"I sure am," Lexie said.

"Am I in trouble?" Charlie asked.

Lexie smiled. "Listen kiddo, your dad's been really worried. When he couldn't find you he called the police."

"He did?" Charlie sounded awed but not afraid.

"Yes he did." Lexie nodded. "We've been searching for you for the last few hours. You scared him pretty good." Lexie stared hard over her shoulder at the father. "But he's *not* angry at you."

"He's not?" Charlie's voice was hesitant.

The father knelt down too, and held out his arms. "No baby, I'm not mad." His voice was softer. "I'm sorry that I shouted. I was scared when I couldn't find you."

At her father's words the girl ran across the room and flung herself into his arms. I saw tears in his eyes as he picked her up. Without another word, he walked straight out the door with the girl.

"Thanks Violet." Lexie gave my arm a friendly squeeze. "I'll go take the Bell family home."

"Bell?" I felt a tingling at the base of my neck and I blinked. "The girl's last name is Bell?"

"Yup." Lexie opened the door. "See you." She gave a wave and left.

I gazed numbly out the window as the handsome man held his daughter and waited for Lexie to open the car door. I automatically locked the shop's door as father and daughter got in the squad car. The man leaned over, put a seatbelt on his child, and pulled her close to his side. There was something about his gesture that had my belly flipping first in reaction, and then with old memories.

"Oh my goddess," I whispered, and my heart began to beat faster in my chest.

He's changed. I thought, studying the man intently. *His hair has turned mostly to silver...that's why I hadn't recognized him.* I stood there and continued to gawk out the window at the man who I'd never gotten over, even though he'd broken my heart seven years ago.

My ex, Matthew Bell, was back in William's Ford.

CHAPTER TWO

The following morning, I was downstairs in the flower shop before sun up. We had a Saturday evening wedding, and words couldn't describe how grateful I was for the distraction of the holiday weekend wedding flowers. Anything that would keep my mind off of Matthew Bell and his child was a good thing.

Plus, I reminded myself, my friend Autumn Bishop was scheduled to arrive at nine a.m. for her own wedding flower consult, and I'd been looking forward to that for a while.

I hadn't managed to get any rest, as I'd spent most of the night wrestling with my emotions. First, I had to deal with the guilty thrill of seeing Matthew again. I'd never stopped loving him. That was a fact. He was literally 'the one that got away'—or more correctly, the man I'd walked away from.

Secondly, I wondered what he was doing in William's Ford. Had he taken a teaching position at the University? Was he visiting his family? Lexie had said she was 'taking the Bells home'. Home where? Was he living in town? It shouldn't matter, and yet it did. Back and forth my mind had gone, from guilt, to shame, to anger, and crazily to hope.

I staggered out of bed, and assessed the damage in the bathroom mirror. My narrow face was too pale, and the circles under my blue eyes were pronounced. However, I couldn't hide in my apartment all day, I had flowers to do. I drug my cosmetics out and got to work, being careful with my makeup and liberal with the concealer.

The cool braided hairdo Marie had done for me was still holding, so I'd fluffed the top a bit and secured the rest into a low ponytail. Other than the hair, it was regular old me today. The only concession I'd made to displaying my crappy mood was the 80's rock I had blasting in my ears, and my purple sweatshirt that read, *I can't adult today*. The snarky sweatshirt was mostly covered up by a green work apron, otherwise I'd never get away with wearing it.

Three hours and three cups of coffee later and the two bridesmaid's bouquets were finished and resting in stands on my work station. All of the boutonnieres were completed, and I'd started on the bride's bouquet. Carefully, I began to build the bouquet, one stem at a time. The bride had chosen well. The red roses, sprigs of goldenrod, orange Gerbera daisies and golden sunflowers were cheerful, autumnal and charming. Humming along with Joan Jett's, "I Hate Myself For Loving You", I tucked in some red hypericum berries, rotated the bouquet and added seeded eucalyptus.

I *felt* my friend let herself in the backdoor, more than I heard her. Autumn's personal energy was vibrant and cheerful. I reminded myself to relax. Otherwise she'd pick up on—

"Violet?" Her hand dropped on my shoulder.

"Hi ya," I said, tugging an earbud out with my free hand. "Be with you in a minute."

"No worries." Autumn considered the work station. "Wow, you got an early start."

"We have a wedding tonight," I said.

"How was your Black Friday?"

"Awesome." I clicked off the music and set the iPod aside. "We broke our sales records."

"That's great!" Autumn said. "Hey, did you know that you're all over the town's website this morning? That Sugarplum Fairy costume was a huge hit."

"Really?" I struggled not to be embarrassed. "I had no idea."

She unbuttoned her royal blue coat and pulled off her gloves. "Did Marie do your makeup?"

"She did."

"Tell me about the lost child you found." Autumn winked and set her coat aside, revealing a bright red sweater.

"How'd you know?" I asked.

"Your picture wasn't the only thing that was on the town's website."

"Aw Jeez." I shut my eyes against embarrassment.

"Meet Violet O'Connell." Autumn deepened her voice. "Mild mannered florist by day—Sugarplum Fairy and witchy hero by night."

"Yeah, that's me." I added another sunflower to the bride's bouquet. "I guess the girl was wandering Main Street hunting for the Sugarplum Fairy. Anyway, I spotted her, and brought her inside. Got her warm and called the police."

"I heard Lexie was the officer that responded."

I tucked more berries in the bouquet. "She was, and she had the girl's father with her." I managed to make that statement casually, and was pretty damn proud of myself.

"Ooh..." Autumn came closer to see the bouquets. "Look at those fall flowers!"

"You can pick one up if you like," I said.

Autumn gently lifted a bridesmaid bouquet. "So, was the father careless, or did the little girl simply wander off?"

I shrugged. "He didn't stay long enough for me to get any details." I secured the bouquet's arrangement with floral wire and set it in a holder to rest my hands.

Autumn sniffed the maid's bouquet. "Well I'm sure he was very grateful that you found her."

"I wouldn't know. He never even said thank you."

"Seriously?"

"He scooped her up and left without a word." I heard the slightly bitter tone and could've bitten my own tongue.

"What's wrong, Violet?"

Damn it. I worked up a smile. "Nothing. I only wanted to get a jump on the flowers for tonight, so I could enjoy the bridal consult with my friend."

"You've been at it a while to get all of this done," Autumn pointed out. "And I can tell you didn't get any sleep last night."

"So much for my under eye concealer," I joked. At my friend's bland stare I added, "I had a hard time winding down after Black Friday."

"Violet, are you okay?" Autumn asked quietly, and replaced the bouquet in its holder.

"I will be," I assured her.

"Talk to me." Autumn put an arm around my shoulders. "You were there for me when I faced my feelings for Duncan."

I leaned into her for a moment. "Do you

remember when I told you about the man from my past?"

"Yes, of course I do." Autumn nudged me to the little consult table. We sat across from each other, she set her purse aside, and waited patiently.

I steeled myself. "The missing child's father, was Matthew Bell."

Her green eyes were round. "Your ex?"

"Yes, my ex." I blew out a long breath. "He's back in William's Ford."

"What did he say when he saw you?" Autumn asked.

"Nothing. I don't even know if he recognized me. Like I said, he scooped her up and walked straight out the door," I reminded her.

Autumn adjusted her glasses. "Your makeup was very elaborate, Violet. He might not have known it was you."

"To be fair, *I* didn't recognize *him* right away." I dropped my hand to the table and Autumn took it, giving my fingers a supportive squeeze.

"He's changed." Her voice had a far-away tone, and her eyes became unfocused. "His hair is all silver now."

Witnessing my friend's clairvoyance first hand had a chill rolling down my back. "What do you *see*?" I asked her.

"Dancing...the Black and Gold Masquerade. The man you danced with that night... he didn't wear a wedding ring, but he also never spoke to you, did he?"

"No," I admitted. "I thought it was sort of cool at the time. Gothic atmosphere, this masked, buff, silver-fox held out his hand and invited me to dance without saying a word..." Suddenly it hit me. "Shit! That was him wasn't it?"

"He recognized you during the Masquerade, but he didn't last night. He was too terrified searching for his daughter." Autumn released my hand and shook herself out of wherever she'd been.

"Can you see if Matthew has been here in town for a while?"

Autumn shut her eyes and concentrated. "I see an old two-story brick house by the University. Pumpkins on the porch... So I'd say he's been here since October."

"I wonder if he's still married," I said before I thought better of it.

Autumn opened her eyes and studied me. "I'm sorry about all this, Violet. Are you alright?"

"No, I'm not," I admitted, my voice shaking. "I never stopped loving him, and this hurts like hell. But I need to suck it up. The William's Ford gossip mill will be exploding about this soon enough, and I don't need to add any fuel to the fire."

"You are allowed to feel hurt and angry," Autumn said. "He cheated on you all those years ago, got some other woman pregnant… then he rolls back into town and tricks you into dancing with him."

I was humiliated just thinking about it. "Damn it," I muttered. "He played me the night of the Masquerade."

Autumn nodded in agreement. "It was sneaky. Would you have even danced with him if you'd realized who he was?"

"Hell, no." *At least I didn't think I would have.*

"He'll come back," Autumn said with

conviction. "To the shop. He'll want to thank you in person for finding his little girl."

"I appreciate the head's up." *He wouldn't catch me off guard this time. I'd be cool, calm and distant as the moon.* I decided. *He would never have any reason to guess now how I felt.*

"I figure he'll show before the day is up. Late this afternoon probably."

"Well then." I drummed my fingers on the table top and considered my options. "I'll be more than ready for him."

Autumn crossed her arms. "You gonna go all bad-ass Witch and turn him into a newt for acting like such a jerk?"

I wiggled my eyebrows. "Oh I'll be *much* more creative."

"You're my hero." Autumn gave me a knuckle bump.

I sat back in my chair and considered my friend. "You know what?" I said. "We're not here to use the hour before I open the shop to talk trash about my ex. We are here to choose your May wedding flowers."

"We can do both." Autumn raised a single eyebrow. "I can multitask."

Her serious face had me grinning. "Let's put it aside for now." I rubbed my hands together to make her smile. "Now, what do you have in mind for those flowers?"

"Well I made a few pin boards, like you suggested," Autumn said, taking her phone out of her purse.

I pulled out my wedding notebook. "Good. What are you thinking?"

"Please don't smack me," she pleaded. "I have lots of boards, and *lots* of pictures."

"Of course you do. Every bride does. What sort of budget do we have in mind for the flowers?"

Autumn cleared her throat. "Ah...Duncan's uncle is paying for everything. The tents for the reception, the music, the food, and the flowers. We tried to talk him out of it, but he wants us to have a perfect day..."

"That's wonderful." I jotted the information down. "Stop feeling guilty, honey. Thomas Drake can afford it."

"Still, I don't want to take advantage of his generosity, so I don't want to go too crazy."

"Noted," I said, dryly. "I'll restrain myself

from doing a bunch of thousand dollar centerpieces."

"I knew I could count on you," Autumn said soberly. She sat for a moment and pressed a shaky hand to her heart. "Gods! I'm getting *married*, Violet!"

"You know, I heard that somewhere..."

"Well I was thinking, since the date is close to Beltane...and I had this vision, white tents on a green lawn, a ceremony in the garden. Maypole ribbons in sherbet colors..." She stopped herself. "And I'm babbling. Sorry."

"You're fine," I assured her, writing as fast as I could. "That's a fabulous idea by the way. A 'Beltane Garden' theme."

"What would it look like if we did a mixture of different flowers, in a rainbow of pastel colors?"

"Pretty." I nodded.

"You know, so it matched each of the bridesmaid's dresses?"

"Sure." I made a note. "What color dresses?"

"All different colors, but probably the same style chiffon dress," Autumn said. "I was thinking pale pink, butter yellow, mint green and sky blue... maybe lilac."

"How many bridesmaids will there be?" I started counting the colors she'd listed.

"Well that depends," Autumn said, taking a deep breath. "Violet, will you be my bridesmaid?"

I dropped my pencil. "Really?"

"Yes really," Autumn replied. "Duncan and I would both be honored if you'd be one of our bridesmaids."

"Of course!" I jumped up to give her a hug.

She stood and hugged me in return. "I'll put you in the lilac dress, of course."

"You'd better," I laughed. "Otherwise it will clash with my hair!"

"I can't imagine doing this without you." Autumn squeezed me tight. "*Promise* that you'll help keep me sane for the next six months."

I swiped a finger across my heart. "I promise. I'll keep you from going Bridezilla."

The back door opened and my mother called out a cheery hello. "What's going on?" she said as Autumn and I stood there grinning.

"I've asked Violet to be a bridesmaid,"

Autumn announced.

"How exciting!" My mother rushed over and gave Autumn a hug. "Let me see that ring!"

Autumn held out her left hand. "Ooh," Mom cooed over the engagement ring. "What sort of stone is that?"

"It's a green sapphire," Autumn said. "I told Duncan I'd prefer a colored stone."

"It suits you. Matches your eyes," Mom said.

"That's what Duncan said when he picked it out."

Bad mood forgotten, I slung my arm around my friend's shoulders. "I'm going to make you the best wedding flowers you have *ever* had!"

"I never had any doubts," Autumn said, laughing and crying at the same time.

"Alright girls." My mother pulled up another chair to the consult table. "Let's talk wedding flowers."

***

The rest of the day passed in a blur. After Autumn left, Mom cranked out the wedding corsages, and we finished all ten pumpkin floral centerpieces by lunch. The deliveryman picked them up and they were on their way to fulfill some happy bride's November fantasy.

The shop was typically quiet the day after Black Friday, so after we cleaned up, I sent Mom home and let Tank come down to the shop. Taking Autumn's predictions to heart, I ducked in the little bathroom in the back and touched up my face.

"The updo Marie did is still hanging in there." I tugged the ponytail holder out, fluffed the bottom of my hair, and slicked on some purple lip gloss. "He played you," I glared at myself in the mirror and proceeded to give myself a stern talking to. "Remember that *and* that he's married. Don't let your feelings get in the way." I practiced a few haughty and disinterested expressions in the mirror and nodded in satisfaction.

Prepared for battle, I sat on a stool behind the work station, sipping at a bottle of water, and blew off the last hour of work. Tank sniffed around the store and eventually curled up under the large tree in the front window. I hummed along with the shop's holiday music, and went over my notes for Autumn's wedding flowers.

The jingle bells on the wreath chimed as our shop's door opened, and I heard the sound of running feet. I snapped my head up and found a familiar little sprite standing in front of the work table.

"You look different today." Charlotte Leigh Bell studied me intently. "Where are your wings?"

And she's alone. Again. I thought. "Hey, Charlie." I mentally psyched myself up for the coming confrontation with her father. "Where's your father?" I asked.

"He's parking the car." She shrugged. "He told me to wait, but I wanted to see you." Charlie barreled forward. "Hey, you have purple tennis shoes!"

"Sure do," I said, while Charlie inspected the purple chucks. "Maybe we should—"

The jingle bells sounded again and Matthew Bell strolled in to my store. "Charlotte Leigh," he said, sounding thoroughly exasperated. "I asked you to wait."

Charlie skipped back to her father. "I wanted to see the Sugarplum Fairy, Daddy."

Matthew shook his head at his daughter and then lifted his eyes, gazing directly at me. He smiled. "Hello, Violet."

CHAPTER THREE

"Matthew." I nodded, even though my heart leapt. I tried for an ice-queen vibe and sent one of those disinterested expressions that I'd practiced his way.

He considered me for a moment, and I studied him back just as thoroughly. Matthew's lashes and brows were still dark, and they set off his honey-brown eyes. His hair was almost all a gorgeous silver. Shiny and thick, it was cut shorter on the sides, and was longer and tousled at the crown. It didn't make him appear older than his thirty-five years, but it did make him stand out. *By the goddess,* I thought. *Tall, buff and handsome. The man was more attractive than ever. It really wasn't fair.*

"Charlotte and I wanted to come in to thank

you," he said, his hand on the girl's shoulder. "For your help yesterday."

"I see." I nodded and stayed seated on the stool. If I stood up, my shaking knees would totally blow the ice-queen act that I was trying so hard to project.

"I didn't recognize you last night." Matthew tried another smile. "Between the fairy costume, the makeup, and the purple wig."

"I wasn't wearing a wig," I said, offended.

"Daddy says your name is really Violet. Like the flower." Charlie giggled. "Is that true?"

"Yes," I said, as Tank wandered out into the middle of the sales floor. He plopped himself between me and the Bells.

Charlie gasped. "Daddy look!" She dove after the cat, and Tank stayed where he was, allowing her over-enthusiastic affection.

"Is the cat friendly?" Matthew asked a bit too late.

I inclined my head. "Usually." I let the threat of that hang in the air.

Tank swung his head around and glared at me. We both knew he wouldn't hurt a child. If anything he'd simply ignore them.

"What's the kitty's name?" Charlie wanted to know.

"Tank," I answered, staying where I was.

Matthew chuckled. "As in, 'built like a tank'?"

"He's a British shorthair," I explained. "They are a muscular breed."

The cat ducked under Charlie's arm as I spoke. He stuck his tail in the air and sauntered towards the back room.

Charlie shucked her red coat and scrambled after him. "Here kitty, kitty."

"Stay where I can see you, Charlotte," Matthew called after her.

"There's so many bows and ribbons!" Charlie's voice floated from the back. "So many colors."

Despite myself I grinned over the child's reaction, and then flinched as Matthew was suddenly standing right next to me.

His eyes searched mine. "It didn't hit me until late last night, that *you* were the one that had found Charlotte."

"Seriously?" My sarcasm was automatic. "Walking into my family's flower shop didn't clue you in?"

"I never even noticed where I was," Matthew admitted. "I was too focused on finding my little girl."

His voice was deep, husky, and skittered right down my spine. Like it always had. I gritted my teeth against my involuntarily reaction.

Charlie ran out on the sales floor, holding a canister of cat treats. "Can I give the kitty a treat?"

"Yes, you can. Make sure he sits and acts like a gentleman first," I said, studying Matthew. The double meaning was crystal clear.

"Okay!" Charlie dashed back, calling for the cat.

Matthew pulled up an empty stool and sat. "Violet, I'm sorry," he said softly, resting a hand on my arm. "It was quite a shock when it finally dawned on me who the Sugarplum Fairy actually was."

"Don't play like this is the first time you've seen me." I shrugged his hand free. "We danced together at the masquerade and you purposefully hid who you were."

"Well it was a *masked* party." His lips curved up slightly. "You were beautiful that night." He leaned a little towards me.

Was he moving in for a kiss? I struggled to maintain my composure.

"But I remembered your temper and figured that if you would have known who I was—you'd have belted me." His voice was a sexy murmur of sound.

"Matthew..." I whispered as he drew nearer. "I wouldn't have done that."

"Oh?" He moved in closer still. "What would you have done?"

"I would have told you to fuck off," I said, politely. "And then I'd have sent you straight back to your wife—or to hell."

Startled, he jerked back. "Violet, you should know—"

"Speaking of which," I cut him off, ruthlessly. "Where was the little woman last night when you lost track of your own child?"

Matthew's face went suddenly blank. "Charlotte's mother passed away almost two years ago."

"What?" I was horrified at his

announcement. "What happened?"

He checked over his shoulder, ensuring his daughter was out of earshot. "Car accident."

"I'm sorry, Matthew." My stomach churned. *Oh my gods!* I thought. *What could I possibly say to the man that would make up for my rude words in the face of tragedy?* I gulped. "I didn't know you were a widower."

"I know that you didn't. And apology accepted." He blew out a breath and sent me a wary look. "I don't recall you being so quick with an apology before."

"Don't get used to it," I suggested. "It's a one time deal." I crossed my arms over my chest. "So now you've moved back to William's Ford?" I asked.

"When a position came open at the University this fall, I accepted it. I wanted to move back home, to be closer to the people I care most about."

"Teaching English Lit?" I asked.

"Yes." He nodded. "The hair is new. I like it."

Caught off guard by the shift in topics I narrowed my eyes. "It's *not* a wig."

Matthew ran a fingertip along the ends of my hair where it rested on my arm. "It's striking. I've never seen a woman with blonde and lavender hair."

It took everything I had not to react to his touch. "What, you're suddenly into hair color?"

"I'm into *your* hair color," he corrected.

"Whatever." My stomach clenched, but I managed to wave his unexpected compliment away.

He chuckled. "I've missed you, Violet."

"Ah, I—" I stammered over the unexpected admission. "I haven't missed you," I lied, folding my hands in my lap.

He slid a hand over mine, and I couldn't stop the involuntary tremble. "No?" he whispered, inching closer.

Practically nose to nose with him I searched his eyes. "Are you flirting with me Matthew?"

"I want to see you again." His voice whispered along my skin. "Spend time with you. Alone. We need to talk."

Even as my insides went haywire, I pulled back. "Do you honestly expect to pick up where we left off, almost seven years ago?"

"No, I don't," he said. "Not exactly."

"What *do* you want Matthew?"

"Violet." He cleared his throat. "There are a few things that I need to tell you..."

"Come back, kitty!" Charlie's happy shout had us jolting apart.

Tank came tearing out of the back room, and Charlie was right behind him. Caught up in the thrill of the game, the cat dove for the front window, and a poinsettia toppled over with a crash.

"Tank!" I said. "You know better. Come out of there!" I went to rescue the potted plant and the cat jumped out of the display window, streaked past me and ran straight at Charlie—and leapt. She caught him, overbalanced at the weight, and landed on her butt. Her gales of laughter had me smiling despite the broken flower pot.

"I caught him!" Charlie sounded proud.

"You sure did," I said, setting the poinsettia on my work station. It wobbled and fell over. "Well shit," I said half heartedly over the plant.

"Daddy?" Charlie piped up. "Were you fighting with the Sugarplum Fairy?"

"No," we answered at the same time.

Matthew stood. "Violet and I were talking."

Charlie's eyes were huge. "Nuh-uh, you were arguing, and she used bad words."

Tank meowed his two cents worth and sent me a feline glare of disapproval.

Damn, I thought ruefully. *Got my chops busted by a cat and an almost-six year old.* I'd never seen the cat take such a shine to a child before. He tended to avoid them. "Charlie." I held out my hand and she climbed to her feet.

"Her name is Charlotte," Matthew corrected me.

"She can call me Charlie," she said, walking over to take my hand.

"Adults argue sometimes," I explained. "Your daddy and I..." I trailed off trying to find the right words. "We used to know each other a long time ago."

"You're friends?" Charlie asked.

"Yes," Matthew said.

"We used to be," I said, giving the girl's hand a squeeze.

"We're trying to figure out if we can be friends again," Matthew said.

"You should say you're sorry for fighting." Charlie's big hazel eyes shone up at her father. Next, they locked onto mine.

Suddenly I wanted to do anything to make her smile. It was almost a compulsion. I shook that feeling off, noticed the time and dove on the perfect excuse to get Matthew Bell out of my shop, *and* the hell away from me. *Before I did something stupid,* I thought. *Like jump right into his arms.* I cleared my throat. "It was wonderful to see you again Charlie, but Tank and I have to close up."

"Awwww!" Charlie's displeasure was loud and long.

I walked to the door. The jingle bells on the wreath chimed as I opened it. "Thanks for stopping by," I said pleasantly, holding the door.

I'm not sure what would have happened next because the judges from the Holiday Happening Committee marched right in. "Violet!" Sharon Waterman, Historic Society member and judge, gave me an enthusiastic hug.

Caught, I could only smile and pat her on the shoulder. "Hello Mrs. Waterman." I nodded at the other two judges. "Mr. Coomer, Mr. Davis."

Sharon stepped back from the embrace but kept my hands, giving them a squeeze. "We wanted to drop by and congratulate you, in person."

The store decorating contest. I thought. *Please don't let it be a runner up prize.*

"Of course the results won't be posted until Sunday afternoon," Mr. Coomer said, "but we needed to make sure that you and your mother as co-owners are both present at the awards ceremony tomorrow."

"Awards ceremony?" I did my best to sound calm.

"Yes, we wanted to inform you that your shop has won first prize for best décor, *and* for most creative use of theme, in our Holiday Happenings Contest."

"Both?" My jaw dropped. "We won first prize in *both* categories?"

"Yes you did." Mr. Coomer nodded.

"Thank you!" I grinned and accepted the handshakes from the three judges.

They filled me in on the details, the when and where for the awards ceremony, and I saw

Matthew zipping up Charlotte's coat. They began to walk towards the door.

"Well, hello Professor Bell." Mr. Davis stuck out his hand.

"Mr. Davis." Matthew shook his hand.

The man knelt down. "And this must be Charlotte?" He held out his hand for the girl too, and she shook it. "Heard we had a little excitement trying to find you last night, young lady."

"Oh!" Sharon Waterman zeroed in on that. "*This* is the child that had North Main Street in a tizzy."

"North Main?" I asked. Our shop was on South Main...*It was a hell of a long walk for a child to make alone, and at night.* My stomach flipped over at the thought of that cute little girl all alone. "Charlie, how did you get all the way up here by yourself?"

Charlie shrugged. "I followed the fairies. They told me where to find you."

Matthew took her by the hand and flashed a bashful grin at the other adults. "We have quite the imagination."

"I didn't imagine it Daddy!" Charlie insisted.

"They told me to follow the lights and the jingle-bells so I did." Her bottom lip pouted out. "It was like magick."

While the other adults had a good chuckle over the girl's comment, I didn't. *The spell,* I thought. *The spell I'd used on Thanksgiving night.* While everyone around me chatted, I tried to remember my exact wording... *Sugarplum spells and silver bells that merrily do ring*...had been the beginning.

"We'll let you close up." Sharon patted my arm. "Congratulations dear. We'll see you and Cora tomorrow." The trio of judges left, and Matthew and Charlotte followed them out. I waved to everyone and locked the door behind them.

"Charlie must be a sensitive," I said, watching as Matthew loaded his little girl in the car. When he shut her door, he caught me staring. In defense, I flipped the sign over to 'closed' and stepped away.

I shut off the lights at the front of the sales floor, ran the closing reports, and deliberated over what had happened. "Somehow my spell called her to the store," I muttered to myself.

"Which shouldn't surprise me. Her father had been fairly open minded when it came to magick."

As if to confirm my realization, Tank gave me a head-butt to the back of my leg.

"Not now Tank. I'm having a crisis." I pulled the work apron off, tossed it over a nearby wall hook and started to count down the drawer.

It took three tries to get it right.

Tank jumped up on the counter to sit beside the register. "Meow," he cried, and spat out a jingle-bell.

I did a double take and clutched the countertop as the room spun around me. "Sugarplums and silver bells." I picked up the jingle-bell. "Matthew has silver hair now. Meaning he could literally be *the* 'silver Bell'. His daughter was looking for the Sugarplum Fairy." I gulped and stared at that little trinket, hard. "And I'd chanted, 'if you need some joy and magick, my call you will hear.'"

My stomach took a nasty pitch. "Could *that* have caused Matthew to act so…smitten today?" I wondered. It was horrifying to realize that my witchcraft had gone so wonky. I'd never had a spell backfire in such a spectacular way before. I'd damn near lured the girl and her father to the shop.

For Witches, ethics and integrity were both vitally important and yet...because I'd worked a spontaneous spell, the results were chaotic. "Like some novice, I didn't consider all of the ramifications of my phrasing." Covering my face with my hands, I groaned in frustration.

The good news was that the spell was destined to end at midnight on Christmas Eve. So I could safely work to *lessen* the spell's unexpected affects on the Bells, and then all I had to do—in theory—was to allow the magick to run its course. And everything should settle down.

In theory, anyway.

CHAPTER FOUR

On Monday, the first prize ribbons for best décor and most creative use of theme in the Holiday Happenings Contest were proudly displayed in our front window. Mom and I, as co-owners of the flower shop, had been awarded the prizes at a short ceremony the afternoon before, and now word had gone out, and the traffic through the store had increased noticeably. Which is exactly what we'd hoped and planned ahead for.

What I didn't expect was the sheer amount of children wanting to know when the Sugarplum Fairy would be making a return appearance. Since I typically worked the afternoon to evening shift on Saturdays, I agreed to take one for the team and redo the character for the next *four* Saturdays. However, in order to pull this off, we needed some help.

Mom and I contacted a couple of witchy friends, and within a few hours we had a schedule in place. The character would be making a return appearance every Saturday until Christmas Eve from two to four p.m., when we were usually slow.

Her visits would also feature the opportunity for posed photos. Ivy Bishop—Autumn's cousin and amateur photographer—showed up to the meeting full of ideas. She suggested that we donate all the profits of her photography to the local animal shelter. All Ivy wanted was to cover her expenses and, in the process, gain some publicity for her blossoming photography career.

Marie Rousseau was also at our meeting, and she was happy to do my makeup again. Besides being a tattoo artist, Marie did event staging and makeup effects professionally, so she was happy to donate her time and talents, after all it was good advertising for her too.

I didn't get nervous until Marie started making noises about switching up my hair and makeup each time. Ivy jumped on the bandwagon saying she wanted to go through my wardrobe to help coordinate my outfits/costume.

After our emergency SPF (Sugarplum Fairy) meeting, as Ivy called it, reality set back in. I did my weekly grocery shopping, came back to my apartment, started the laundry and cleaned house. I enjoyed living above the shop for the past five years. The bathroom and bedroom were nicely sized, and there was even a dedicated space for a stackable washer and dryer in my hallway.

The living room/kitchen was divided by a breakfast bar, and the area rug over the old wood floors was a modern pattern of gray, black and lavender. In the living room, the gray couch had touches of my signature color on the pillows. Plus, the plain white kitchen cabinets were a good foil for the pops of purple that I'd added with accessories and dishes.

Ivy wasn't scheduled to raid my closet until later, so I plopped down on the couch. "What in the world have I gotten myself into with four more appearances?" I wondered, surveying my little purple palace.

The remnants of the banishing spell I'd cast the night before were still on the coffee table. I'd taken advantage of the dark of the moon and scattered hydrangea blossoms around my miniature cauldron. The gray candle I'd burned to neutralize my previous spell's effects was spent. The jingle bell Tank had gifted me with was inside the cauldron next to the candle holder. I felt confident that any unintended fascination my first spell might have caused had been safely nixed by last night's spellwork.

With that under control, I decided that now was as good a time as any to decorate for Yule. I hauled the totes out of the tiny second bedroom that I used for an office and got to work. My little balcony overlooked Main Street and was already draped in evergreen garland and white lights.

To jazz it up a little more, I decided to add another strand of lights—in purple. I tossed my coat back on and worked the additional lights into the garland. I stood on the balcony and gauged the Main Street traffic below me. "Shoppers will be able to spot us from a block away with the addition of the purple lights." I shivered in the cold wind, let myself back in the sliding door and got to work on the rest of my decorations.

Tank sat on top of the totes, flipping his tail. I patted him on the head and began the set-up of my own apartment-sized tree, strategically placing the four foot artificial evergreen on top of a tall round table in my living room.

I sang along with the holiday music that was playing on the radio, ignored the cold front that was roaring through town, and decorated. The artificial garlands were fluffed up and added over my windows. I plugged the garlands in, and the tiny white lights beat back the dark. My Yuletide accessories were placed around the apartment, and I was finishing up the final touches on my own tree as Ivy arrived. I opened the door to a gust of wind that had me shivering.

"Hi ya, Vi." She gave me a one-armed hug.

"Hey Ivy." I shut the door behind my favorite Gothic girl.

"That's a cool tree!" Ivy went for a closer inspection.

"Thanks." I bent, plugged the tree lights into a timer and plugged it in.

"I like the purple and white ornaments." Ivy ran a finger over a poufy sheer bow I used as a tree topper.

Tank came barreling out to see who had arrived. He ran to Ivy, head butted her leg, and made her chuckle.

"Hey big guy." Ivy patted the cat on the head.

"I was thinking about making some hot chocolate," I said, snapping the lid shut on the tote that had held all the ornaments. "Do you want some?"

"That does sound good." Ivy draped her black Peacoat over a chair and revealed her *Nightmare Before Christmas* sweater.

I carted the totes back to the second bedroom and went to the kitchen. While I started the cocoa, Ivy sat on a barstool and filled me in on the latest gossip.

"Did you hear that Leilah Drake Martin is moving out of town with her mother over holiday break?"

I set two mugs on the counter. "Really?"

"Yeah." Ivy smiled. "She failed a bunch of classes this semester, and word is that old man Drake has finally had enough of his daughter's drama—and cut her off without a cent."

"That would be a good thing for Autumn and Duncan." I dropped a few marshmallows in the mugs. "I admit I was worried about her conjuring up all sorts of trouble for them with the wedding."

Ivy nodded. "I know Leilah is Duncan's cousin, but I'm not afraid to say that I want that bitch gone and out of William's Ford."

"Agreed," I said. "We don't need that sort of magickal chaos in town."

"What's with the banishing spell?" Ivy tilted her head towards the spell components still on the coffee table.

"Oh, it's only a little work to cover my bases," I assured her. I served the hot chocolate, and had no sooner joined Ivy at the island when there was a knock on the door.

"You expecting someone else?" Ivy asked.

"No." I frowned at the door as the knocking continued. I set my untouched drink down and went to answer it, only to discover a little elf in a red winter coat.

Charlotte Leigh Bell was alone and on my doorstep. Again.

"Charlie!" Horrified, I quickly pulled her inside and out of the wind.

"Hi!" She smiled, sunnily. Her blonde hair was sticking out from under her striped hat, and a small backpack was slung over her shoulders.

Ivy rose to her feet. "Hey there, kiddo."

"Hi!" Charlie grinned at Ivy. "I like your sweater."

"I like your face," Ivy said, making Charlie giggle.

"What are you doing here?" I asked the girl.

"I came to see you." She pushed her cap back. "Aren't you happy to see me?"

"Of course I am," I said, my mind reeling. "But sweetie, *how* did you get here?"

"The school bus." Charlie dropped her backpack on the floor. "Do you have any cookies? I'm starving!"

"The school bus?" I repeated.

"Yeah, the school bus." Charlie started to unzip her coat.

"*This* is the little girl you found the other

night," Ivy said, narrowing her eyes.

"Yes it is." I picked up Charlie's discarded coat and draped it over a chair.

"Violet, the school bus doesn't run to this part of town," Ivy said.

"I know." I exchanged concerned glances with Ivy. "Charlie, how exactly did you get downtown?"

"I asked Mrs. P to bring me here instead of taking me home." She pulled off her hat and squealed in delight when Tank made his way straight to her. "Hi Tank!" Charlie knelt down and the cat burrowed right in her arms.

"The school bus driver dropped you off here, instead of at home?" I tried to keep up with her.

"Sure." Charlie smiled, innocently. A huge pink bow attached to a headband decorated her wispy hair. With her bubblegum pink sweater and gray corduroys, she seemed absolutely angelic. "I just asked her really hard," Charlie said, "and she did what I wanted."

"You just asked her really hard..." Her words had me catching my breath. *What if the child was more than a sensitive? What if she had power?* "Charlie," I said in a soft, coaxing tone.

"Look at me." I gently cupped her chin in my hand and raised her eyes to meet mine. I did a light scan, wondering what I'd find.

Our eyes locked, and I felt a jolt of magick go all the way to my toes. Charlie began to giggle, and I allowed my eyes to go unfocused so I could see the child's aura. It was a glowing vibrant pink with clouds of white.

"By the old gods," I breathed. Charlotte Leigh Bell not only had magick, she was carting around a level of power I'd *never* experienced in a child so young.

"Oh, I see pretty lights," Charlie said, staring up at me.

"What colors do you see?" I asked.

"Green." Charlie's laughter bubbled up and made me smile in reaction. "Violet you have green all around you. Like leaves."

The child was reading my magickal energy. I was aligned to the earth element, and only one other person in my life had ever told me that they'd seen leaves and flowers all around me—my maternal grandfather, Ronald Lewis.

"She can see your aura," Ivy said from behind me. "Damn, Skippy."

"When I look at you I see pink with white clouds," I told Charlie.

"You see pink and clouds?" Charlie thought that over.

"Yes I do." I released her and stepped back. Fortunately there were no traces of the earlier sugarplum spell lingering on the child. I breathed a little easier realizing that it wasn't *my* magick that had called her back today.

Ivy knelt down and held out a hand. "Try again, Charlie," Ivy said. "What do you see now?"

Charlie took the offered hand, peering at Ivy Bishop. "Yellow," she said after a moment. Yellow light all around you, like the sun."

"Maybe she's a natural..." Ivy spoke carefully, avoiding the W word in front of our guest.

A Natural Witch, I thought. It wasn't unheard of for people to discover they had abilities even when no other family member possessed magick…But typically it didn't begin to manifest until their teenage years. "She's awfully young to be displaying that much talent."

"Autumn did," Ivy said. "Remember, we found out after she moved here that her dad had bound her powers when she was little, because it upset her mother."

"That's right." I considered the young girl who grinned at us.

"My mom always said that I ran her ragged when I was little..." Ivy smiled over that. "But I've never run across a *natural* with this much juice."

"I like juice!" Charlie announced.

Ivy titled her head, assessing the child. "Who taught you how to see the colors, and to 'ask really hard', Charlie?"

"Nobody." Charlie's bottom lip poked out. "Mrs. Gruber gets confused when I ask her really hard, and then Daddy gets mad at her."

"Who's Mrs. Gruber?" I asked.

"The housekeeper," Charlie said.

Ivy placed her hand on Charlie's shoulder. "Don't you think Mrs. Gruber's going to worry that you didn't get off the bus?"

"Nah." Charlie shrugged. "She's probably asleep on the couch."

Charlie's casual response made my stomach

turn over. "Does Mrs. Gruber usually forget to meet you at the bus stop?" I asked cheerfully, as if it were no big deal.

"Yeah," Charlie said. "I mostly walk home by myself."

"By yourself?" It took everything I had not to explode in anger at the housekeeper's lack of regard for a young girl's safety.

"Can I have a snack?" Charlie asked with a grin.

"Sure." I ushered the girl to my kitchen island and boosted her up on a barstool. I gave her my hot chocolate and a few cookies. While Charlie called happily to Tank, I stepped back and spoke to Ivy. "I have no way to contact her father. I don't know where he lives, and I don't have his cell number."

Ivy shook her head. "What *do* you know?"

"All I know is that he teaches at the University." I blew out a long, frustrated breath.

Ivy nudged me with an elbow. "I bet Bran would know how to contact a professor on campus. Or we could call Lexie again."

"Ask Bran to track down Matthew Bell—he's in the English Department, and let him know that Charlie is here."

Ivy nodded, whipped out her cell and called her brother. I kept a smile in place and played hostess, while Charlie demolished the cookies, drank all my hot chocolate, and cooed over Tank, who'd jumped to the other stool to be near his new favorite person.

"Thanks, Bran." Ivy tapped on her screen. "Hey Lexie," she said next.

My eyes shot over to her while Ivy spoke on the phone. "Oh yeah?" Ivy said. "So the department, the school *and* the bus service has been trying to find her for about an hour?"

Oh wonderful. I rolled my eyes to the ceiling. *The William's Ford Police department was going to be at my door for the second time in a matter of days.*

CHAPTER FIVE

An hour later, armed with the Bell's address, I found myself driving Charlie home. It had taken a bit of time to straighten everything out. Understandably, Matthew was extremely upset to have discovered his daughter unaccounted for, once again.

Bran Bishop had tracked down Matthew, who had been on the phone with a concerned principal at Charlie's school, and one very distraught bus driver. The search for his daughter had been called off, and Bran had spoken to Matthew personally, to inform him where Charlie was, *and* that she was safe.

Matthew had called to thank me for "finding" Charlie, and further surprised me by asking for an hour so he could settle things with his housekeeper. Even though I wasn't an intuitive like Ivy, I was sure he'd fired the woman. I could only hope the bus driver wouldn't lose her job as well.

"Am I in trouble?" Charlie asked as we drove across town.

"I'm pretty sure you are." At my words, the radio in my car suddenly went to loud static. I slanted my eyes towards her. *Somebody was upset.*

"Why?"

I clicked the stereo off. "For starters, you should have gone straight home after school, and secondly, you shouldn't have manipulated Mrs. P."

Charlie scrunched up her face. "What's 'nipulated mean?"

"It means that you made Mrs. P do something she wouldn't have done on her own," I said.

Charlie tugged her hat over her eyes.

"That was wrong, Charlie."

She pushed the cap up a bit, and hazel eyes regarded me solemnly. "It was?"

"Yes it was." I eased to a stop. "You and me,

we need to have a long talk about this *asking really hard* thing that you do."

Charlie's shoulders hunched defensively. "Okay."

I wondered, as I drove on, how to best explain the rules of magick to a child. *I'd have to talk to Matthew as well,* I realized. *Try and make him understand Charlie's unique skills.* I could only roll my eyes at that. *How in the sweet hell did one start that particular conversation with a non-magickal parent?*

"How come your hair is purple?" Charlie suddenly wanted to know.

"Because I like it this way."

Charlie reached over and ran her fingers through my hair where it was draped over the sleeve of my winter coat. "I like it too," she said, happily. "Could you make *my* hair purple?"

"You'll have to ask your father about that."

At the mention of her father, Charlie's smile shifted into a pout.

I pulled up in front of an elegant, brick two-story home. The older house was in the Federal Revival style. The brick was a soft aged red, the roof a smoky gray, and the shutters and front door were painted in glossy black. As soon as we climbed out, Charlie latched onto my hand.

"Don't leave me," she said piteously. We'd only started up the brick sidewalk when the front door opened.

"Charlotte Leigh Bell." Matthew crossed his arms over his chest. "You are grounded for the rest of your life."

"Matthew." I inclined my head, coolly. "We really have to stop meeting like this."

"Violet." His brown eyes assessed me. "Please come in." He held open the door and I walked in.

"Thank you." I nodded as Charlie clung to my hand.

He shut the door behind us. For a moment he considered his daughter, and eventually he bent down and hugged her. "Charlotte, what has gotten into you lately?"

"I'm sorry, Daddy," she said contritely.

"Do you have any idea how frightened I was when the school called?"

The child shrugged. "Mrs. Gruber wasn't at the bus stop so I went to go and see Violet instead."

Matthew ran his hand gently over the girl's head. "Mrs. Gruber won't be a problem anymore."

"Was she sleeping on the couch again?" Charlie asked, unzipping her coat.

Matthew did a double take.

"Charlie tells me that she's been walking home *alone* from the bus stop most days," I said pointedly.

"*What?*" Matthew sounded horrified.

"I think you and I should chat," I said. "There are a few things you need to know."

"Can Violet stay?" Charlie asked her father.

"Young lady," Matthew's voice was stern. "You can go directly to your room." He pointed towards the staircase.

"Yes, Sir." Head hung low, Charlie trudged up the steps and out of sight.

My lips twitched, but I managed to keep a sober expression.

"Can I take your coat?" Matthew asked courteously.

"Thank you," I said, and unbuttoned the eggplant colored wool coat. *How polite we are,*

I thought. The formality made me twitchy, but I played along.

He hung the coat on a hook by the door and ushered me into the living room. I almost cringed at the uninspired décor. Khaki walls, brown sofa, tan leather club chairs, and a beige carpet. It was all perfectly bland. Even the fireplace had been retiled with a taupe colored tile. I chose the couch, it looked the most comfortable.

With a sigh, he slumped in a chair across from me and leaned his head back. "Thank you for finding her."

"I didn't." My words had his head snapping up. "*She* found me. Apparently she walked down Main Street, saw that I wasn't in the shop, and figured out to go around the back of the building. Then she climbed up the steps to my apartment door."

"My god." Matthew ran a shaking hand through his hair. "When I think what could have happened...I can't believe the bus driver was so careless!"

"Don't blame the bus driver," I said. "Charlie can be quite *persuasive*. Surely you must know that."

"What do you mean?"

"I mean that your daughter has gifts. Certain talents that you may not be aware of."

"No, I had her tested," he said, sounding tired and defeated. "She didn't qualify for the academically gifted program."

"No, no. I didn't mean academically gifted." I shook my head. Out of the corner of my eye I spotted a collection of framed photos on the mantle and a struggling little plant. I studied the pictures and tactfully refrained from commenting on the lack of photos of his deceased wife.

"What do you mean?"

I didn't answer him immediately. My attention was caught by a large group picture in an ornate silver frame. The group photo featured a younger Matthew, his sister and parents, with what had to be his aunt, uncle and cousin all gathered around an older couple—probably his grandparents. "Family portrait?" I asked, pointing at it.

Matthew scowled at me. "Don't change the subject."

"I'm not, really." I stood and went to the mantle. "Matthew, did Charlie's mother have any genealogical links to the founding families of William's Ford?"

His back stiffened. "No, her entire family was from the New York area."

"Are you sure?" I asked, and picked up the droopy little potted plant. It was an African violet. *How ironic,* I thought.

"Yes, I'm sure," he said. "What does Veronica's family have to do with this situation?"

"I've never asked you before, but what is your mother's maiden name?"

"Abbott," he said going very still. "Mom's maiden name is Abbott."

I recognized the name and struggled to keep my voice even. "And where did your mother's family originate from?"

"Massachusetts. The Danvers area."

Bingo, I thought, and ran my fingertips over the wilted, yet still fuzzy, leaves of the plant. "Matthew, have you ever noticed that when Charlie—"

"Charlotte," he corrected.

"—gets angry," I continued as if he hadn't interrupted. "That things fall over or break?"

He frowned. "What do you mean?"

"Does the radio go off station, do the channels change on the television spontaneously, or does your cell phone act up if Charlie's in a temper?"

He shifted in his chair. "Yes it does." His golden-brown eyes became intense as he thought it over. "How could you have possibly know that?"

"How long have these electronic disturbances been going on?"

"For the past few years," he admitted. "Is something wrong?" His voice went up in alarm.

"No, not at all." I tried to assure him. "Matthew, do you remember several years ago, when I told you about my family line, my legacy?"

He leaned forward in his chair, resting his elbows on his knees. "Yes. Your mother's family had links to the Salem Witch trials. You used to dabble with Wicca or something...it didn't bother me."

Offended, I pulled my shoulders back. "I

never *dabbled* with Wicca." I met his eyes, and let him feel my resolve. "I am a Witch. That's completely different."

"Sure." He spread his hands. "Whatever term is more politically correct these days."

The slightly condescending air made me want to throw something at him. Instead I focused my attention on the poor, neglected plant in my hands. Silently, I sent it some healing energy.

"What does your interest in witchcraft have to do with anything?" he wanted to know.

"Do you remember what happened the last time we fought? That day I left?"

"The windows broke," he said quietly. You didn't slam the door, but the front windows cracked when you left."

"What else?" I prodded.

"The flowers in the window boxes all suddenly withered and died." He studied me intently. "I'd never seen anything like it."

"No, you wouldn't have. I was very careful and restrained around you."

Matthew grinned. "Violet, you were many things but *restrained* wasn't one of them."

I narrowed my eyes. "I'm not talking about sex, you idiot. I'm speaking of magick." I held the plant up to eye level and considered it. The African violet had noticeably plumped up and was now vibrant and robust, where before it had been withered and dying. I tilted my head towards it. "I bet you've never seen anything like *this* before, either."

"What in the world..." Matthew's voice trailed off.

I smiled down at the plant. "You can do it," I whispered. The plant quivered, and a little bud burst open revealing a ruffled white blossom. I shifted my attention from the plant to Matthew, gauging his reaction.

He blinked and his jaw dropped. "How...how'd you do that?" he stammered.

"Well I sure as hell didn't do it by *dabbling*."

Matthew jumped to his feet. "Oh my god!"

"Is it starting to sink in, Professor Bell?"

"I always thought the stories about the founding families of William's Ford were simply old wives' tales," he said, turning a little pale.

I took a breath, and prayed for patience.

"Aren't you the one who used to say that there was often a kernel of truth in the old faery tales, myths and legends?"

"So what does all of this have to do with Charlotte?"

Gently, I slid the potted plant back on the mantle. "Magick, like other talents, can be hereditary. Sometimes it skips a generation and can pop up where you least expect it."

"Meaning?"

"I'm betting Charlie's gifts come from your mother's family line. The Abbotts."

"What *gifts*?" He demanded as a few beads of perspiration appeared on his upper lip.

"Matthew, in the simplest of terms Charlie can influence people—make them do what she wants. She can manipulate them both mentally and physically by using her natural abilities."

"No she can't!" Matthew snapped.

His reaction angered me. "How many nannies, babysitters and housekeepers have you gone through?" I asked on a hunch. "How many gave into Charlie, because they simply couldn't seem to resist her, or follow your rules?"

"Coincidence," he said.

I walked over and poked him in the shoulder. "That little girl has more raw power than half of the adult practitioners I know. At first I thought she was a Natural Witch, but since your family line includes the Abbotts, Charlie may have basically won the equivalent of the hereditary magickal lottery."

"I'm not going to listen to this any longer." Matthew's face was an angry red. "I think you should leave."

"That kid needs help—needs to be magickally trained, before she hurts someone, or herself!"

"That's ridiculous!" He took ahold of my arm and began to steer me towards the foyer.

"You know I'm right!" I yanked away from him and glared.

He snatched my coat from the peg and tossed it to me. "Leave. Now."

"Fine!" I snarled. "But the next time Charlie gets it in her head to go and wander off, you better hope to whatever god is listening that she doesn't decide to *influence* someone into taking her on a cross-country trip."

"Get out." His voice was flat and angry.

I marched past him. "Give your mother a call," I suggested as I tossed the front door open myself. "Do a little digging in the roots of your family tree. You'll see."

I stomped down the sidewalk and the front door slammed shut behind me. I whipped my car door open, tossed my coat in and pulled the door shut behind me. I started the car, checked over my shoulder for oncoming traffic, and pulled away from the Bell's house with an angry squeal of tires.

CHAPTER SIX

A miserable week and a half had passed since I'd seen or heard from Matthew or Charlie. The days had been busy and long, and my current work day had been capped off by a semi-hysterical bride who'd wanted to change her wedding bouquet at the last moment.

Thanks to the Bridezilla's demands I ended up working a good hour *after* we'd closed. However, her bouquet did look better. Now, burgundy ranunculus popped along side the creamy white roses and cedar greenery.

Deliberately, I passed my hand over the bouquet and called on my magick. I linked into the element of earth, and the roses opened up a tad more. Satisfied with how it had finally turned out, I whispered a charm over the bouquet, ensuring that the flowers would hold and stay lovely throughout the wedding day. Finally, I added the bride's bouquet in the box with the rest of the finished wedding flowers.

With a sigh of relief, I backed out of the cooler, rolled my tired shoulders and began to clean up my work station. Five minutes later, I made my way up the back stairs to my apartment.

Tank came trotting out, stopped and considered me. I shed my coat, tossed it towards a chair and went directly to my fridge. I selected a bottle of wine and poured myself a large glass. Sitting at the kitchen island, I took a sip, sighed, and indulged in a private sulk. The only light in the room was coming from the matching evergreen garlands above the sliding door to the deck and the living room window, and that suited my mood perfectly.

I rubbed my forehead. Now that I was home, I could admit that I missed them. Which was ridiculous, and probably inappropriate. I'd only seen Matthew and Charlie a few times...how could I miss them?

The more I thought about it, maybe it was for

the best that I hadn't seen Matthew for the past ten—eleven days. Because I had no idea what I would've said to that man *if* he had crossed my path. I wasn't sure what hurt me more...his cavalier dismissal of the Craft, his wide-eyed shock at having it proved to him, or his stubborn refusal to believe that his daughter had any ability.

"First he flirted, then he freaked." I took another swallow of the wine.

"Meow?" Tank leapt to the island. He walked straight to me and gave me a none too gentle head butt.

I began to laugh when he rubbed his face against mine. "Hey big guy." I took comfort from my familiar. He sat beside me, leaning against my shoulder, and my stomach began to growl. "So should we heat up leftovers, or order takeout?" I asked him.

Tank's answer was a deep, throaty purr.

A loud thump on my door had me glancing over my shoulder in surprise. Before I could move to answer it, the door burst open. Ivy Bishop came in carrying a large handled bag. "I knew it!" she cried. "Sitting up here in the dark having a little pity party for yourself." She shoved the door closed with her boot, and simultaneously the timer for the tree kicked on illuminating the apartment.

"Ivy," I blinked at the invasion and the lights. "I didn't expect you tonight."

"Never fear! The official photography Elf has arrived!"

"Well now I can relax," I said dryly.

"I had a hunch you needed a friendly ear, *and* food." She peeled out of her coat and carried the take-out bag to the kitchen island. "Figured you'd go for shrimp and mixed veggies."

Tank perked up at the word *shrimp*. He immediately began to sniff the takeout bag. I quickly hauled the cat back before he could pull the bag over. "Tank gets a little wound up when you say the S word out loud," I warned her.

Ivy leaned over and dropped a loud kiss between the cat's ears. "Well, it's a good thing I got two orders."

I couldn't help it, I started to laugh. "Anybody ever tell you that you're incorrigible?"

"I get that a lot." Her green eyes were serious, but smiling. "But regardless, I *knew* you needed witchy company, and Chinese food tonight."

"As usual, your intuition was spot on." I patted her shoulder. "I'm glad you dropped by."

"Your name's been stuck in my head all afternoon," Ivy admitted. "I got the impression that you needed cheering up, and a flyer for takeout ended up taped on my dorm room door. When I get intuitive information and synchronistic events like that, I don't fight the signs."

I set the cat on the floor and got up to go fetch a few plates. I slid them on the bar top while Ivy took the food out of the bag. "What would you like to drink?"

"I'll take some of that white wine." Ivy said, setting a carton of rice on the counter.

I added a wine glass in front of her plate. "So how are your photography classes going?"

"Great," Ivy said. "I'm glad the semester is almost over, and I am really excited to be graduating in May." She plucked out a fat shrimp, leaned over and offered it to Tank, who pranced off with his treat.

"Well, the cat is happy now." I poured the wine and joined her at the island. We divvied up the food and dug right in.

"Call me an intuitive," Ivy said after a few moments. "But I'm betting the reason you've been in a funk for a while is because your talk with Professor Silver Fox didn't go very well."

I choked on my rice. "Professor *Silver Fox*?"

Ivy thumped me on the back. "That's what the female students on campus are calling him." She wiggled her eyebrows. "You neglected to mention that your ex is *smoking hot*."

"Good god," I managed. "I don't think I ever told you that Matthew and I used to be a couple."

"You didn't. But the campus grape vine is filled with juicy information about the sexy widower." Ivy leaned her arm on the counter. "So, how'd the 'your daughter's a Witch' talk go?"

I decided the conversation called for more wine and topped off my glass. "Not well."

Ivy smirked. "Not well, as in—I don't believe you? Or not well, as in—the power of

Christ compels you! Be gone foul demon—type of thing."

My lips twitched. "He tossed me out, but refrained from the latter."

"Well that's something," Ivy decided, swinging her foot. "Tell me everything."

I sighed, gave up, and filled her in on my last conversation with Matthew. "...and I haven't heard from him since that day. Which proves that he's an intolerant idiot, after all."

"Maybe not." Ivy reached for her wine. "I heard his final assignment for the English Lit class was to write a paper on *The Crucible*, with an emphasis on the historical, and social ramifications of the Salem Witch Trials."

"He did?" I dropped my fork in sheer shock. "Really?"

"Yeah, he did," Ivy said.

Had he spoken to his mother's relatives after all? I wondered, and cleared my throat. "Maybe he'll actually learn something when he reads those papers." I tried to tell myself it really didn't matter. "You know, I don't usually order from the Jade Dragon, but this food is really good."

"Feast well my friend. You'll need your strength for the dark days ahead," Ivy said, deadpan.

Her comment had me chuckling. Her good humor was infectious and I enjoyed the meal and the camaraderie. Afterwards, we ended up in my room while Ivy raided my closet for a different Sugarplum Fairy outfit for the next day.

"Oh my goddess!" Ivy waved a purple and black corset. "*This*!"

I studied the satin fabric with the flocked black roses, vines and thorns. "Figures you'd like that one. It's got the Gothic vibe you'd go for."

"Yeah it does." Ivy pulled a long black tiered broomstick skirt off a hanger and held it next to the corset. "I'll bet you'd stop traffic in this."

I titled my head as I considered her words. "Ivy, this whole Sugarplum Fairy thing is for the kids in town, not to 'stop traffic', as you so elegantly put it."

"Hmmm." Ivy tapped a finger to her lips.

"Last week we did casual," I reminded her. "My dark jeans, a lilac and black sweater and my purple chucks. It was comfortable."

"I agree. The subtle pastel-goth style went well with your hair worn in two pigtails and the more playful makeup," Ivy said. "But...we need to switch it up. Trust me." She dove back into my closet and pulled out a long sleeved, black lace shrug. "You could toss this over the corset."

I took the shrug. "That could work."

"Besides, Professor Silver Fox *will* show up tomorrow afternoon. I have a hunch Charlie's been nagging him brainless." Ivy grinned. "He's gonna cave in and take her to see you again."

"You think so?"

Ivy handed me the corset. "I *know* so."

I held up the flocked satin and considered my reflection in the mirror. "Tomorrow, eh?"

"Looking hot is the best revenge, Violet." Ivy appeared beside me in the mirror. "You'll have him losing his mind, *and* the power of speech when he sees you in this little number."

A slow smile started to spread across my face. "I like the sound of that."

"Trust me." Ivy winked. "Now, let's talk

jewelry."

***

The Sugarplum Fairy made her third appearance. I pulled my long hair away from one side of my face and secured it with a fresh purple rose. Taking her clues from the outfit, Marie did a forest fairy theme makeup. She painted little black rose vines from the corner of my eye and down across my exposed jaw and neck. The makeup was a bit darker than I usually wore. The eyeliner was smoky and smudged, and my lips were painted a dark mauve.

We'd been crazy busy with holiday sales all afternoon. Decorated wreaths, tree ornaments, and potted poinsettias had been the hot ticket items. My younger brother, Eddie was manning the front counter, *and* between sales he'd been trying his hand at flirting with Ivy Bishop.

"Eddie, she's seeing someone," I tried to break it to him gently.

Eddie leaned an elbow on the counter and sighed over Ivy as she chatted up a young family. "She's great."

"You're only sixteen, she's almost twenty-two," I said. "She's too old for you anyway."

I followed his gaze. The younger camera-toting Witch was wearing a Santa hat, with black fur trim of course. Her jeans were tucked into tall boots, and her red sweatshirt said: *I'm not short. I'm just a tall Elf.*

"Hey Sugarplum Fairy!" Ivy waved me over. "The Whittier kids want a picture."

I left him mooning over Ivy and went to sit in a chair by the white display tree. I smiled for pictures with a trio of young siblings. The oldest, the only girl, stood by my side. She was currently rolling her eyes at her youngest brother who was unhappy that there were no 'sugarplums' out today.

"If you want sugarplums," I told the children, "go right next door to my friend Candice's shop. She makes cakepops in every color and flavor you can imagine."

"She does?" The middle child, I'd estimated him to be about five, leaned in.

The youngest boy, a blue-eyed heartbreaker sat in my lap. "Does she have cookies?" he asked.

"She was making gingerbread men this morning," I said, and watched their faces light up.

"Mama, can we go to the bakery?" the girl asked.

The children's mother finished filling out her email information. "Gingerbread does sound good," she agreed.

Ivy handed the mother a claim number for the photos. "Check the website tonight for the pictures, Mrs. Whittier," she said.

The jingle bells on the wreath chimed as the door opened, and Charlie and Matthew entered the flower shop. I stood, and had the supreme satisfaction of watching the man's jaw hit the floor.

Ivy nudged me with an elbow. "Told ya." She aimed her camera at him, and clicked. "I'll email you a copy of that one," she said under her breath.

Charlie skipped over. "Hi Ivy!" She giggled as Ivy pointed the lens down and took a few quick pictures of her.

"Gotcha." Ivy lowered her camera, and her

silver pentagram necklace caught the light. She stuck out a hand to Matthew. "Hello, Professor Bell, I'm Ivy Bishop."

Matthew glanced down at the pendant, and grinned at the sweatshirt. "Charmed." He shook her hand.

"Hi Violet!" Charlie raced to my side and grabbed my fingers.

I couldn't help but smile. "Hey kiddo," I said.

"You're so pretty today!" Charlie swung my hand back and forth. "Isn't Violet pretty, Daddy?"

"Hello, Matthew." I nodded politely.

"Violet." He cleared his throat. "We dropped by to pick up a poinsettia for the house."

"We have plenty," I said casually, and did my best not to sound smug over his reaction to seeing me. "What color were you wanting?"

"Color?"

"Of poinsettia?" I reminded him.

Matthew scanned the shop. "White would be nice."

Of course he'd go for white, I thought. *Goddess forbid the man put something with color into his life.*

Taking his cue from the conversation, Eddie walked over and handed Matthew a potted poinsettia with gold foil around the pot. "How's this one?" he asked.

"That's fine." Matthew nodded and followed Eddie to the check out counter.

"You have a purple rose!" Charlie's comment had me glancing down. "It's purple, like your hair."

"Roses can be purple?" The oldest of the Whittier trio asked.

While Matthew paid for his purchase, I walked Charlie and the children over across the sales floor and pointed out the bucket of silvery-lavender colored *Ocean Song* roses that were in the cooler.

"Hey kids," Ivy called out. "Why don't we all go over to the bakery and see what cookies Candice has conjured up today?"

The trio of siblings cheered and Charlie looked to her father. "Can I go too, Daddy?"

"I'll keep an eye on her," Ivy volunteered. "We'll only be gone for a few minutes."

"I'll help." Eddie finished slipping a plastic

sleeve over the plant and handed it to Matthew. Before I could blink my brother had zipped over to stand at Ivy's side.

Matthew gave his permission, and Ivy took Charlie firmly by the hand. Eddie held the door open and herded the Whittiers out the door and their happy chatter faded away. Which left me alone in the shop with Matthew.

Matthew stayed by the front counter and I remained by the cooler. Neither of us said a word, even as he continued to stand there and stare.

I propped my hands on my hips. "Why are you really here, Matthew?"

CHAPTER SEVEN

An expression came over his face. One that I recognized from years before, and it had me literally bracing for impact. Without a word he walked over, yanked me into his arms and kissed me. Not a chaste kiss. A hot, open-mouthed kiss that swooped in and claimed my lips and tongue, *and* had my head spinning. Just like old times.

With a muffled groan, I kissed him back. In the past, whenever he'd put his hands on me, any good sense or inhibitions I'd had would fly right out the window. *But maybe it shouldn't have,* some sane part of me realized. When his hands roamed down over my backside, I snapped out of his sensual spell. "Stop, stop," I said, pulling free.

Matthew slid his hands from my hips and eased back slightly. "I knew it."

"What?" I whispered as his eyes searched mine.

"The passion." His voice was low, his breathing a little ragged. "It's still there."

Angry at myself for my instantaneous response to his kiss, I pushed him away. "First you throw me out of your house, and now you show up to my shop a week and a half later and kiss me? You've got some nerve."

"I wanted to see you again," he said softly.

"We're in the middle of my shop for goddess sake!" I snapped. "A customer could have walked in. Your *daughter* could have walked in!" I stomped to the central table, snatched up a mirrored tray and checked my face. Lipstick was all over my chin. Mortified, I tried to wipe it off with my fingers.

"Use this." A snowy white handkerchief was waved in my direction.

I snatched the linen square away from Matthew and tried to wipe up the smeared lipstick. When he stepped closer, I held up a hand. "Back off."

He stepped cautiously forward against my warning. "I want you, and I know you still want me." He trailed a fingertip over my lace covered shoulder.

I shuddered. "Wanting you was never the problem."

"Then there's no problem at all." His quiet words hit me like a ton of bricks.

"I'm not some breathless twenty year old who'll fall at your feet." I reminded him. "Not anymore." I tossed the handkerchief in his general direction.

He caught it neatly. "I haven't got the patience for twenty year olds. I'd rather have you."

So it's all about sex, I thought and felt my heart crack. Deliberately I set the mirrored tray down before I gave in to the urge to throw it at his head. "Well, now that you've satisfied your curiosity, I'd like you to leave. I have a business to run."

"We need to talk." His voice was brisk.

I hesitated at the change in the tone. "About what?"

"There are things I need to explain to you. I

would have the other day, but..." he trailed off.

"Is this about Charlie and her heritage?"

"Charlotte," he corrected. "Yes, it is. But there's more." He wiped my lipstick from his mouth.

The intimate gesture went straight to my gut. I told myself to ignore it and scowled at him instead. "Matthew, what's really going on here?"

"It would be best to discuss the situation in private," he continued. "Can you come to the house tonight? Say around nine?"

"I'm not interested in a booty call, Matthew."

"No, that wasn't my intention at all," he said perfectly composed.

"So says the guy who just wiped my lipstick off his mouth."

Matthew's lips twitched, but he managed to stop the grin. "I'm serious, Violet. I owe you the truth, and we do need to clear the air—" he was cut off from saying more by Ivy, my brother, and Charlie's return to the shop.

"I got gingerbread men, Daddy!" Charlie announced, holding up a small bakery box.

"Wonderful." Matthew smiled at his

daughter, and accepted the box. He sniffed it dramatically, making the girl giggle. "Smells good."

"Ivy says I should eat the feet first so they can't run away," Charlie said solemnly.

"Or the head," Eddie chimed in. "That way they can't see how to escape."

"Gross!" Charlie laughed at my brother.

"That may be a little intense for a five year old." Matthew frowned at them.

Ivy slid her own bakery box on the counter. "The days leading up to Yuletide are the darkest ones of year." She patted Charlie on the head and lowered her voice dramatically. "The Wild Hunt fills the air, the frost faeries are up to mischief, and ghosts roam the earthly plane..."

Charlie clutched Ivy's hand. "Have you ever seen ghosts, Ivy?"

"Yes," Ivy answered simply.

"Were they scary and mean?" Charlie wanted to know.

"One was," Ivy said to the girl. "But the other was kind and she helped me and my friend."

"Really?" Charlie's eyes were huge.

"Really," Ivy replied.

"On that note," Matthew reached out and tugged his daughter to his side. "Charlotte and I should be leaving." He handed her the box of cookies. "We need to go get a tree."

"Christmas tree!" Charlie shouted happily.

It was already mid-December. They were getting an awfully late start on decorating, I thought. "There's a farm on the outside of town, they sell fresh cut trees," I suggested. "McBriar Farms." Internally, I congratulated myself on how calm and professional I'd sounded.

Matthew nodded and picked up the poinsettia from the counter. "I know where that is, we bought pumpkins from them on Halloween."

"Thanks for stopping by," Eddie said to the Bells.

"Happy Holidays." Matthew nodded to everyone and ushered his daughter out the door.

***

Mother Nature seemed to have gotten in the spirit of the season, and we had light snow showers for the rest of the afternoon. Foot traffic on Main Street had dwindled down to zero by closing time. Debating with myself over Matthew's invitation, I went back upstairs to my apartment and stripped out of the Sugarplum Fairy outfit.

"He must have spoken to his mother and had his family's magickal heritage confirmed." I wiped the rose vine off the side of my face with makeup remover and a cotton ball. "What else could it be?" I asked my reflection.

"Meow?" Tank jumped to the bathroom counter and nosed around in the basket that held my cosmetics.

"He admitted this was about Charlie's heritage, Tank. But why all the secrecy?" I frowned at my face in the mirror and laughed at the elaborate eyes, with no makeup at all from the eyes down. I shook myself off and redid my foundation, blush and powder. The dramatic eye makeup I left as it was.

Somewhere in the middle of redoing my face I realized that I *was* going to Matthew's house tonight—only to talk. I was simply too curious not to. I brushed out the hair style and tossed a knit ivory sweater over a pair of jeans. The ivory sweater was slouchy, worn off the shoulder, and it complimented my pale blonde hair, making the lavender streaks pop. As a final touch, I tied a choker around my neck. The ribbon was a deep indigo, and a little crescent moon charm dangled from it.

After dinner, I schlepped around the apartment and tried to relax. When I caught myself checking the clock for the fourth time, I tossed up my hands. Eventually I settled on the couch and watched the falling snow. I told myself it was like meditating, watching the snowflakes drift down until it was time for me to leave.

Felling a little more mellow, I bundled myself in a coat and a scarf and found that while the light snow was sticking to the grass and tree branches, the streets were too warm for the snow to cause too much trouble. I carefully went down the back steps, scraped the soft snow off my windshield and enjoyed the magick of a wintery night.

I arrived at the old brick house on time and parked at the curb. I stood beside my car, gazing up and down the street. Decorated trees twinkled in windows and white icicle lights, or vintage style multicolored larger bulbs accented the lines of the roofs. I rotated in a slow circle, noting pine roping with tiny white lights on neighboring porches, lit wreaths that hung on windows...all of the typical holiday décor.

This historic neighborhood took pride in its holiday decorating, there was even a holiday light tour held on the twenty-second of December every year. Every house in this old established neighborhood was beautifully adorned. Every home—except for the Bell's house.

In contrast, the Bell's house was somber, and the only light was the standard issue fixture on the front porch. My inner florist balked at the undecorated home. "And you're stalling," I said to myself. "Mentally decorating everything instead of going in and finding out what he wanted to talk to you about." I squared my shoulders and walked to his door.

I knocked briskly and the door opened to a more casually dressed Matthew than I'd seen since he'd come back to town. His navy sweater made the silver in his hair shine, and his jeans were old, worn and snug. *Don't even go there,* I thought, yanking my eyes away from his butt. *He wanted to talk. Let's find out what the man has to say.*

"Violet." He smiled. "I'm glad you're here."

A short time later I was sitting on the brown couch while Matthew stood by the hearth. A six foot, undecorated spruce now sat in front of the curtained picture windows. The poinsettia he'd purchased sat alone in the middle of a dining room table. The living room was still a bland, neutral nightmare. The only saving grace was the crackling fire that he'd built in the brick fireplace.

"Is Charlie down for the night?" I asked conversationally.

"Yes, *Charlotte* is." He emphasized her name. "Why do you keep calling her Charlie?"

"Because when I first met her she told me her name was Charlotte Leigh." I shrugged. "It sounded like Charlie and it sort of stuck in my head. Besides, it suits her."

"She's insisting on being called that now," he said with a sigh. "Even at school."

"Charlotte is an awfully serious name for a

little girl. Did you name her after Charlotte Bronte or something?"

He smiled. "Yes."

"Figures. Bronte always was a favorite author of yours." I smiled and tried to pretend that the polite conversation wasn't making me tense.

Matthew ran a hand through his hair and blew out a long breath. "I'm trying to decide where to begin," he admitted, and tucked his hands in his jeans pockets.

I'd never seen him fidget before. "Are you okay?"

He nodded, swallowing nervously.

"Did you speak to your mother's family about your heritage?" I asked, trying to get the ball rolling.

"I did, yes." He gestured to the large family group photo on the mantle. "My maternal grandfather, Xander Abbott, had quite a bit of information actually."

I leaned forward. "What did he tell you?"

"Our family lineage can be traced all the way back to the late 1600's. The Salem Village area."

"Which is modern day Danvers." I nodded. "You said the other day that your mom's family hailed from Massachusetts."

"I never knew that I had ancestors who were accused and imprisoned during the Witch trials." He blew out a long breath. "Or that there were other relatives who had gifts."

"So Charlie isn't the only one?"

"No." Matthew stared at the floor, clearly miserable. "She's not the only one who's been able to influence people. But she is the most recent."

For some reason my heart began to beat faster. Something was very wrong. "What is it? What are you so afraid of?" I asked.

Matthew began to pace in front of the fireplace. "When Charlotte was two years old she was hospitalized for bacterial pneumonia. While she was there, they ran many tests...blood tests."

My heart started to beat loudly in my ears.

"It was then I found out..." His voice was so low I strained to hear it. "Charlotte is not my biological child."

The impact of his statement had me falling

back on the couch cushions. "*What?*"

"Once Charlotte was out of intensive care, Veronica broke down and confessed to me that Charlotte's actual father was Zack Abbott."

"Your *cousin*, Zack?" My eyes felt like they were going to pop out of my head. "You're saying that Veronica cheated on you with Zack seven years ago?"

"All those years ago, Veronica and I were friends," Matthew explained. "Friends only. She had broken up with Zack, you and I had that huge fight. She and I bumped into each other at a bar and had way too many drinks together. In the morning when I woke up, she was beside me in the bed."

"You slept with her," I said, flatly.

"She told me we'd had sex, but I couldn't remember. I'd blacked out." Matthew walked over, sat beside me on the couch. "A couple of months later when she told me she was pregnant—and that I was the father, I believed her."

"But you aren't," I managed, even as my mind whirled.

"No." He took my hand. "Veronica also

confessed to me that nothing happened between us that night. She made it all up to try and make Zack jealous."

He hadn't cheated on me after all! Was my one clear thought.

"In truth," Matthew said quietly. "It wasn't until *after* we were married that we'd actually had sex for the first time." A dull flush rode up his neck at the confession.

"I see." I struggled to maintain a polite tone. "So she knowingly manipulated you?"

"Yes she did."

"Well that takes a special kind of bitch," I muttered. "Why?" I asked him. "Why would she do that to you?"

"She said that she wanted a safe and good life for her and the baby, and that I could provide that. Zack was always in trouble, remember?" Matthew let go of my hand, stood and began to pace again. "A DUI, bar fights, possession, or gambling debts, he always skirted the edge...Somehow managing to sweet talk his way out of his troubles. Whether it was with his parents, a lawyer, or a judge."

I went over to the mantle and pulled down

the family photo. There they all were, Xander and Melissa Abbot—Mathew's grandparents. His mother Stephanie, his father Ian, Matthew and his sister Peggy; all arranged on the right. On the other side of the photo stood his mom's brother Jason Abbott, his wife Lisa and their only child, Zack.

"So that would make Charlotte a second cousin to you," I thought out loud.

"No," Matthew said firmly. "She *is* my daughter. Genetics be damned. *My* name is on the birth certificate, and I've loved that little girl since the moment she drew her first breath."

"How many people know about this?" I asked gently. "The truth about Charlie?"

"Five people," Matthew said, rising to his feet. "The doctor who ran the tests. My parents, me, and now you."

"What about Zack?"

"He's dead," he said with no inflection. Matthew took the family portrait from me and replaced it. "There was an accident. He'd been drinking and using drugs."

"His parents?" I asked.

Matthew sighed, clearly miserable. "Zack's parents are divorced now, they're both alcoholics. That's no sort of life for a child."

"No, it's not," I agreed. "When did the accident happen?"

Matthew met my eyes. "Two years ago."

*And Charlie's mother had died in a car accident two years ago as well...*Suddenly, hideously, all the pieces fell together. "Zack and Veronica died in that car accident together, didn't they?"

"Yes." Matthew drew a shaky breath. "Veronica had left me and abandoned Charlotte. She and Zack were running off when they died."

CHAPTER EIGHT

The silence in the living room was profound. I leaned against the mantle and let it all sink in. Everything he'd revealed to me had my heart aching and my head spinning. I suddenly flashed back to the last time I'd been in his house.

"So the day that I tried to talk to you, and told you to search your family tree to find out more about Charlie's gifts...you weren't mad because I'd brought up the subject of witchcraft."

He shook his head. "No, I wasn't angry about that."

"But you were afraid," I said, feeling sympathy for him. "You're terrified that someone will find out about Charlie's biological father and try and take her away, aren't you?"

"Yes," he agreed. "I was also afraid for Charlotte. It upsets me to think that she could actually manipulate and coerce people the same way Zack had. She's only a child. She has no way to understand the consequences of her actions."

"She's young, and to her it's all a fun little game." I reached out for his hand and gave his fingers a squeeze. "Let me work with her, Matthew. I can help teach her the rules of the Craft and make her understand the right way to use her gifts."

"I think that would be the wisest choice," Matthew said solemnly. "I'm trusting you with my daughter, Violet."

"She's blessed to have you," I said and meant it. "I won't betray your trust."

"Thank you." His shoulders dropped in relief. "I'll want to be as discreet about this as possible."

"I don't want to alarm you, but Ivy Bishop knows that Charlie has abilities. She's seen them in action. Ivy assumed that Charlie's abilities most likely came down somewhere from the family tree. Which is true."

"Ivy is a Witch as well? I mean, I saw the pentagram, who could miss it?" He rubbed his forehead as he thought it over. "But I thought that was simply a gothic fashion statement."

I smiled at him. "Don't underestimate her. Ivy is *very* talented, her whole family is."

"Wait, isn't she related to Bran? Bran Bishop from the University library department?"

"Yes. That's her brother."

"Are you telling me that their entire family are..."

"Witches." I smiled at him. "You can say the word out loud. No one's going to arrest you. Also, the cop who helped you search for Charlie is Lexie Proctor-Bishop, she's Bran's wife."

"The police officer is a Witch too?" Matthew shook his head. "But they all seemed so normal."

"They are *normal*," I huffed out. "I'm going to let that comment slide, as you've been dealing with a lot recently, but don't push it."

"I apologize. I didn't mean to offend."

"You can make up for it by filling me in on what you found out about *your* family legacy." I sat on the hearth, patted the space beside me, and tried to encourage him to talk.

"My grandfather told me that both his father and his brother Saul, had powers." Matthew sat down next to me. "Grandpa said that his brother Saul was a politician—and in his words—had the gift of gab. Saul was the mayor of his home town, and a fine one according to Grandpa."

"And your great-grandfather, what were his gifts?"

"According to Grandpa, his father Seth was a 'water witcher'. He divined where to dig for wells and so forth."

"I'm familiar with the term," I said. "Did your great-grandfather use metal rods or a forked willow branch to dowse?"

Matthew faltered. "I have no idea. I'll have to ask."

"And your grandfather?"

"Grandpa Abbott was a veterinarian, he's retired now. But I've never seen anyone who could work with animals like he could."

"Well, there you go. With the Abbott family

ties to Salem village, and your great-grandfather being a dowser, no one will question where Charlie got her powers. And good news? Not everyone in your family had issues with their gifts."

"Good point."

"There is an entire community of Witches here in William's Ford who will be happy to help your little girl," I said. "Don't worry. We watch out for our own."

"Thank you," Matthew sighed.

He looked exhausted and I wanted to comfort him, but wasn't certain if that was my smartest move. I sat there helplessly for a moment, unsure of what to do about the rest of his confession. "I should probably go," I said, rising to my feet.

"What?" His head snapped up. "Why are you leaving? Didn't you hear everything I told you?"

"Of course I did." I walked into the foyer for my coat. "I'd like a little time to process it, that's all."

He followed me into the foyer. "Come back tomorrow, for supper," Matthew said. "I know

Charlie would love to see you, and maybe you could start working with her."

I buttoned up my coat. "I have a few deliveries in the morning, I suppose could come by around three."

Matthew reached out and turned me to face him. He dropped a light, chaste kiss on my mouth. "Thank you. For everything. I'll see you tomorrow."

I stepped back and gave him an easy smile, even though it cost me. "Goodnight."

He held open the door for me. "Drive safe."

I drove home slowly, thinking over everything that I'd learned. My heart once broken at the thought of his betrayal, began to mend with the realization of his innocence. When I thought about Charlie, I had to swallow past the lump in my throat.

I'd always loved him...and always would. I'd faced that a long time ago. But now I was perilously close to adoring him for everything that he was doing to protect a child that he considered his own.

***

For the past few years I'd been dropping off elaborate holiday centerpieces at the Drake mansion the weekend before the sabbat of the Winter Solstice. As per usual, Thomas Drake, the family patriarch, had requested traditional arrangements of evergreen, fresh holly and mistletoe. He had also ordered two tree topper bows this year and I had tossed a few spools of various holiday ribbon in the van, along with an emergency supply of decorations and several strings of lights, even extension cords, in case he required any further decorating.

Knowing the family's preferences, I was stocked up on more natural items such as pinecones, sprays of decorative berries, silk red birds, twigs, and both fresh and silk evergreens branches and roping. I knocked on the back door, and was surprised when Duncan Quinn, Autumn's fiancé, answered the door instead of the housekeeper.

"Violet!" He reached out, took the big box from me, and waved me inside. "Uncle Thomas has been expecting you. Come in!" His bright blue eyes were happy and when he smiled, I did too. No doubt about it, my friend had bagged herself a very attractive man.

"I have extra stuff in the van in case we need more supplies," I said as Duncan tugged me along with him. But it ended up that they didn't need anything else. Autumn and Duncan were already busy adding fresh greenery to the various fireplaces and tables in the mansion. Autumn had all the Drake men; Duncan, his cousin Julian, and even Thomas working on decorating the home together, for Yule.

I bit my lip to keep from some inappropriate giggles at the three men racing around at Autumn's directions. I placed the pair of centerpieces in the formal dining room, chatted with Autumn, who was doing a fine job decorating, and handed over the tree topper bows to Thomas. I ended up talking to him about the budget for his nephew's and Autumn's wedding, while Julian Drake climbed a ladder to add the tree topper to the large family room tree.

The elegant man placed the streamers one by one and with precision. Duncan began ragging on his cousin about hurrying up, and not being such a tight-ass. To my shock, Julian made a cheerful yet anatomically impossible suggestion to Duncan as he sang along with the holiday music playing on the stereo.

"Watch your language gentlemen," Thomas suggested.

"Boys," Autumn warned them. "Play nice or I'll zap the both of you."

"He started it," the men said, simultaneously.

Autumn and Thomas began to laugh. The atmosphere inside the home was so relaxed, cheerful and *different* as compared to years in the past that it made me very hopeful for the family.

I arrived at Matthew's house at three, psyched myself up, and knocked on the door. I waited, but no one answered. I knocked again and heard the sounds of running feet, and Charlie greeted me.

"Hi Charlie." I automatically checked for her father. "Where's your dad?"

"Hi!" She grabbed my hand and pulled me inside. "Daddy's in the garage. He's trying to find the Christmas ornaments."

I glanced towards the living room. One

strand of lights had been added to the tree, and the little bulbs twinkled off and on in red. The lights appeared to have been thrown on haphazardly. Stepping into the living room I saw that a half dozen paper snowflakes were only on the bottom branches. *Poor tree,* I thought.

Matthew's voice carried in from the back of the house. "I can't believe it!"

"Daddy!" Charlie shouted. "Violet's here!"

Matthew came around the corner and stopped. He carried a few strands of outdoor lights, but that was all.

"Problem?" I asked.

"The ornaments for the tree are missing. I've searched everywhere," Matthew said. "I'm not sure if they got lost in the move or what happened to them."

"We aren't gonna decorate the Christmas tree?" Charlie's voice wobbled.

"I guess I'll have to try and go to the store." Matthew rubbed his forehead "But this late in the year, I don't know what I can find..."

Charlie began to cry. Frustrated vibes poured off of Matthew, and I took matters in my own hands. "Don't panic," I said. "I have some odds and ends in the floral van that should do the trick."

"You do?" Matthew sounded surprised.

"Grab your coats," I told them both. "We'll haul it in and get to work."

A short time later, Matthew and I unloaded all the extra decorating supplies that I hadn't used at the Drake's mansion and spread the boxes out across the living room floor. Charlie sat in the middle of everything, gazing around in wonder. "It smells like Christmas," she said.

"Charlie, go get your paper snowflakes," I suggested. "Those are special and we'll put them back on the tree last."

"Okay!" she raced to the tree and took the paper ornaments down. "What are you going to do with this stuff Violet?"

"Make some Yuletide magick." I wiggled my eyebrows at the girl.

"But we don't have any ornaments," Charlie said. "How can we decorate the tree?"

"You'll see," I said, unwinding a string of white lights. "I can make one bad-ass rustic holiday tree out of all these supplies."

Matthew's eyes were huge. "I'm suddenly a little afraid."

"Ha!" I tossed my head. "I'm a floral designer, babe. Stand back and prepare to be impressed."

An hour later and the Bell's tree was trimmed out and lovely, if I did say so myself. While Matthew and I had strung the white lights through the branches, Charlie sat on the floor and cut out more paper snowflakes. Once the lights were in place, I took flocked twig branches and silk berry clusters and worked them throughout the spruce, filling up empty spaces. Next, I strung burlap ribbon through the branches like rope garland, and Matthew tied red ribbons onto a couple dozen pinecones. I had both of them hang those as ornaments, while I cleared off their mantle, layered pine greenery and branches of fresh holly on top and worked the set of red lights through it.

I took the half dozen little silk cardinals and pointed out to Charlie where to put them, so the red birds would stand out on the tree. Up and down the step stool she went, placing each bird with help from her father. When she was done we added Charlie's white paper snowflakes and they filled in the tree, adding a touch of whimsy.

While Matthew called in an order for pizza, I pulled out the large spool of burlap ribbon and another of red velvet. I perched on the edge of the big leather ottoman and tied up a two layered bow for a tree topper.

Charlie watched it all with wide eyes. "How did you learn to do that?"

"My mom taught me," I said around the chenille stems I held between my teeth.

I threaded the chenille stems through the ribbon loops, twisted them tightly and fluffed the bow. I attached it to the top of the tree, demonstrating to the little girl how to work the streamers into long curls down the sides.

It was starting to get dark outside when Matthew at last plugged the tree and the mantle lights in, making Charlie gasp in delight. "Oooh, it's so pretty!"

"The paper snowflakes are my favorite." I rested my hand on the girl's shoulder. "You make good snowflakes kiddo."

"It's one bad-ass rustic holiday tree," Charlie

repeated.

I snorted out a helpless laugh at Matthew's reaction to his daughter's comment, and began to stack the boxes.

"The pizza will be here in forty minutes," Matthew said. "Lets get this all cleaned up before—"

"Perfect," I cut him off. "I have twelve feet of pine roping in this last box. Between that and your old outdoor lights we can add a little something to the outside of your house."

"Well, I—"

"As the town's acting Sugarplum Fairy, I should point out that you're the *only* house on the block without any outdoor holiday lights, Professor Bell." I shook my head. "It's shameful."

"Shameful," Charlie parroted my words.

"We can keep it simple," I tried to assure him. "If we wrap the pine roping in the colored lights we could drape the garland over and around your front door."

"Can we, Daddy?" Charlie jumped up and down. "Can we? I want the outside of our house to be pretty too!"

Matthew studied his daughter, then shifted his eyes to me. "Alright," he said. "I did notice an outlet on the front porch. I'll get an outdoor extension cord from the garage." He walked off towards the back of the house.

"You're such a trooper," I called after him.

Charlie ran to put her coat on. "Violet, can we put ribbons on the garland too?"

"Sure," I said. "Go grab that spool of red ribbon."

"Okay!" Charlie dashed off. "I want lots of bows!"

"Not sure how your father's going to feel about that." I shrugged my own coat on over my blue sweater and gathered up the box with the pine roping.

"I can ask him really hard..." she began.

"Charlie," I said in a warning tone.

"Oh." She frowned at me. "Is that man...manip..." she struggled over the word.

"Manipulation," I said. "And yes, it is."

Charlie thought it over. "Maybe I could just say, *please*."

"There you go." I pressed a fingertip to the end of her nose. "It is a magick word after all."

CHAPTER NINE

The Bell's once tan and bland living room had been transformed. Now, red lights twinkled on the mantle amidst a mixture of fragrant greenery, and the rustic tree illuminated the picture window of the living room. While a fire crackled merrily in the grate, the three of us devoured the pizza. Afterwards, I gathered up the mistletoe from the last of my emergency decorating supplies, tied a bow on it, and hung it above the front door.

"Violet?" Charlie asked.

I stepped down off the kitchen chair. "What's up, buttercup?"

"Why do you hang the toe above the door?"

"Mistletoe." I picked up the chair and carted it back to the kitchen. "Because it's a magickal plant of Yule, and it will bless the house with love and peace."

Charlie checked the kitchen carefully. "Is Daddy still outside?"

"Yes, he's hauling all the empty boxes back to my van." The girl seemed so serious, I wondered if she was in trouble.

"Would you come live with us?" she asked. "You could teach me to make the flowers, and I could take care of Tank."

My heart stuttered in my chest. "I have a job Charlie, at the flower shop. I can't be your housekeeper."

Charlie frowned. "No, not like Mrs. Gruber. I love you. I want you to stay with me always."

I couldn't think of a single thing to say to that. The special little girl had wound her way into my heart in such a short amount of time.

"I think I'm going to ask Santa Claus about this," Charlie decided.

Oh dear gods, I thought. Matthew came back in through the kitchen door and Charlie scampered away.

"Something going on?" he asked.

I shook my head. "Do me a favor, and keep

that kid away from any Mall Santas...I have a feeling she's going to start *asking* for things no one is ready for."

"I don't know..." Matthew took my hand and gave it a squeeze. "You might be very surprised at what I'm ready for."

We spent a pleasant evening together. Matthew talked about the classes he was teaching at the University and to my amazement, he wanted to know all about the flower shop. Charlie lay under the tree, staring raptly at it until she finally fell asleep.

"She's out," Matthew said of his daughter, as he sat in one of the leather chairs.

"Decorating for Yule is a big job." I nodded.

"Yet, in one afternoon, you've managed to make this house feel magickal. This is the first time since we've moved in, that it has felt like home," Matthew said.

His words caused a warm fuzzy feeling in my chest. But I tried to keep it light. "I'm a florist. Can't stop myself from decorating. It's a sickness."

"It's more than that," Matthew met my eyes. "It's a gift, and one of the things I've always loved about you."

Loved? I thought. Suddenly nervous, I looked away. *Don't jump ahead girl,* I warned myself. *It's only an expression.*

"I'll take her to her room and tuck her in." Matthew rose to his feet. "Will you stay?"

"Sure, I'll wait until you get her settled," I said.

While Matthew took Charlie upstairs, I went to sit on the hearth. I stared at the flames and waited for him.

He padded into the room quietly and walked over. He hunkered down so we were eye to eye. "Violet, I don't want you to go."

I smiled. "I should head home. It's been a long day."

"No," he reached out and cupped the back of my head. "I want you to stay, and be with me tonight."

His words made my heart leap, and my stomach clench. "Matthew," I murmured. "I'm not sure that's a good idea."

"Yes it is," he tugged me closer. "I'll show you."

The kiss started out as soft and testing, but

didn't stay that way for long. Our tongues met and my hands dove into his hair. The next thing I knew, he pulled me into his arms. I wrapped myself around him and was lost. We'd always had chemistry, and even after seven years apart, it ignited.

Our clothes were gone in moments. There would be no tender coming together. This was all passion, all fire. We wrestled across the floor, both of us straining to kiss and to touch the other. For seven years I'd longed for him. Now, having him in my arms again, I didn't want to wait even a second longer. He rolled me under, I wrapped my arms and legs around him. "Now," I whispered in his ear. "Right now, Matthew!"

He thrust home, and I bit back a shout of joy. He covered my mouth with his and we went crazy, together.

Afterwards, we lay on the carpet before the fire. Matthew trailed kisses down my throat, over my shoulder and across the sleeve of floral tattoos on my right arm. "This is beautiful," he said.

I reached over and with a fingertip, pulled his

face up so I could meet his eyes. "There was a time, you didn't think so," I reminded him.

"I was a fool." Matthew shifted his attention and began kissing his way across my breasts. "Do you have tattoos anywhere else?" he asked casually.

"Well, if you hadn't been in such a rush to set a land speed record," I teased him, "maybe you would have noticed."

Matthew braced himself over me on his elbows and narrowed his eyes. "Is that a challenge?"

I wriggled my hips, and felt his reaction. "Maybe."

He dropped a sizzling kiss on my lips, but to my disappointment he stopped and stood. He stared down at me, silently holding out his hand. I took it, and he tugged me to my feet. As soon as I was upright, he began steering me back towards the couch. His hands were all over me, and he whispered a naughty suggestion as his mouth cruised across my jaw.

I felt the cool leather of the large ottoman hit the back of my legs. "Is that thing sturdy enough?" I asked.

"As a matter of fact," he said, "I had this fantasy of you and I testing it out a couple of days ago."

I smiled against his skin. "Pretty confident of yourself, eh Professor?"

Without warning, he spun me in his arms. Before I could blink, he arranged me face down over the ottoman. I gulped when he knelt behind me and nudged my legs farther apart. He pressed his weight down, and I moaned at the contrast of the smooth, cool fabric against my breasts, and his warm chest against my back. He guided my hands to grip the sides of the ottoman, and wrapping his hands over mine he held me gently in place, and slid inside.

I groaned as my feminine muscles clenched around him. I tried to move, but between Matthew holding my hands and his weight on me, he was completely in control, and I loved it.

He began to roll his hips slowly, and the leisurely tempo had me gritting my teeth. He trailed gentle kisses over the back of my neck and shoulders, but still, he never increased his pace.

"Matthew!" I pleaded, straining back against him.

"More?" He stopped moving altogether and I was left squirming in frustration. "Are you sure?" His voice was a low growl, and it made me want him desperately.

I nodded my head *yes*, and he lifted his chest from my back, releasing my hands. He pressed one of his hands firmly into the center of my shoulders to keep me in place. I held my breath, struggling to hold still as he began to thrust his hips faster. Now his strokes were deeper and more intense.

"God, there's no one like you." He pressed his chest to my back again. "You always could make me crazy," he growled in my ear.

I twisted my head back, straining to kiss him. "Go a little crazier," I dared him.

And he did.

I woke up on the sofa in Matthew's arms. He'd tossed an afghan over us and I sighed in contentment. Reluctantly, I peered up at the grandfather clock as it chimed the hour, and groaned. "I need to go," I said, patting his arm.

He tugged me back so he could see my face.

"You don't have to leave."

I kissed the underside of his jaw. "Unlike you, I'm not on winter break. I have to open the shop in the morning. Besides, it's not a good idea for me to stay the night with Charlie upstairs." I rolled to my feet and got dressed quickly. Standing in my jeans, I hooked my purple bra into place, and glanced over to discover him watching me intently.

"The only reason I'm letting you go is because we aren't alone in the house." He rose to his feet and the blanket fell, leaving him standing gloriously naked in the firelight.

"Wow," I said as my heart began to beat faster in my chest. "Standing there like that, you're not making it any easier for a girl to leave." I tried to keep my tone light.

"This wasn't a casual hookup." Matthew slipped on his jeans, left them unsnapped, and reached for me.

"I wouldn't have been here with you like this, if I thought it was." I pulled my sweater over my head, and evaded him. "I do need to go," I said, moving quickly. Knowing full well that if he put his hands on me again we'd end up right back on the floor, going at each other for a third time. I shoved my feet inside my shoes and headed for the foyer. "Goodnight, Matthew," I said, grabbing my coat and opening the door.

"Violet," he called after me. "I hope you will believe it when I say that I *never* stopped loving you."

I froze, and the coat slipped out of my suddenly numb fingers. I turned slowly around to face him. "What did you say?"

"I love you," he said, walking to me.

"You do?"

He took my hands. "I love you Violet, and I always have."

His words, so close to what I'd regularly thought about him, had my throat closing and tears spilling over. "Matthew, I—"

"We've already lost seven years," he interrupted. "I don't care if I'm moving fast. I don't want to wait anymore." Matthew kissed me firmly. "In a perfect world, I'd carry you up those stairs, make love to you until dawn, and that would be that. We'd be the family we should have always been."

"But it's not a perfect world," I reminded him.

"No, it isn't." He kissed my forehead. "However, I'm willing to put the time in and prove to you that I could make it damn near perfect."

I opened my mouth to try and respond, but it took me a few tries. "So you want to be with me?" I finally managed to say. "To build a relationship and to build a family?"

"Yes," he said, kissing the back of my hands. "We can go slow, if that's what you need."

I laughed despite myself. "Matthew, you're saying that like we didn't just have crazy sex all over your living room."

"I'm trying to prove to you that we have *more* than sex between us." His eyes were intense. "Give me a chance. Give us a chance. I want your magick in our lives."

Sugarplums, spells and silver bells, I thought. "I've always loved you, Matthew. There's no magick on earth that could ever change that simple fact."

"Violet," he murmured and lifted me off me my feet. He kissed me with an intensity that left me breathless, and I heard the door shut as he carted me back to the living room.

"I love you." I kissed him with all the emotions I'd had bottled up for seven years. "Always have, always will," I promised, running my hands over his bare chest.

"Hey." He set me down and captured my hands. "I meant it. We can take it slow from here on out."

"Fabulous," I said, and pulled my sweater over my head. "So, we'll do it *slowly* this time."

A light came into his eyes as the sweater dropped to the floor. He cupped the back of my head and pulled me close. "Violet, I love you. Always."

"Show me," I said.

With soft and lingering kisses Matthew and I made love again. Slowly and tenderly, whispering all the while how much we loved one another.

EPILOGUE

The Holiday Light Walk was in full swing, and I shuffled along the sidewalk holding hands with Matthew while Charlie skipped in front of us. During the past week, we'd spent as much time together as possible. Which wasn't easy, considering this was one of our busiest times at the shop. However, it was well worth the effort.

"Are you ready for Yuletide dinner with the O'Connells?" I teased him.

He smiled down at me. "Sure, what could possibly go wrong? The woman I love and her mother are both Witches, you have two teenage brothers, and your step-father is a retired fire fighter."

"He only gets his axe out for special occasions," I said soberly, and then giggled at Matthew's wince.

Charlie pranced back to us. "Is it time to go to Cora's house?" she wanted to know. "I want to eat the turkey and stuff, and Cora made real sugarplums!" Charlie chattered on. "And I want to see Kevin and Eddie again!"

"We only have to walk a little further down the street to get to Karl and Cora's house," I assured her.

"Charlotte, you're going to be on your very best behavior tonight," Matthew said as we made our way down the street. "No asking *really hard* for anything."

Charlie was the picture of innocence in her red coat. "No Daddy," she said meekly. "I'll be good."

It took everything I had not to snort with laughter. "My mother can more than handle anything Charlie does," I said as we started up the driveway of my parent's house. "Don't worry."

"What about your brothers?" Matthew said, while Charlie raced for the front porch with a jubilant shout. The door opened and the sound of jingle bells filled the air. My mother stood there all smiles, welcoming her inside.

"Kevin and Eddie are capable practitioners." I patted his arm consolingly. "Charlie won't influence them."

"Your brothers are Witches too?" Matthew's eyes were round. "I'd never considered that possibility."

"Besides," I said tucking my tongue in my cheek. "If I were you, I'd be more worried about what spells and tricks they'll teach Charlie."

Matthew stopped dead on the front steps. "Tell me you're joking."

"Afraid not." I kissed him on the mouth. "Face it Professor, your life is going to be very interesting from now on."

The End

ABOUT THE AUTHOR

Ellen Dugan is the award winning author of twenty five books. Ellen's popular non-fiction titles have been translated into over twelve foreign languages. She branched out successfully into paranormal fiction in 2015 with her popular "Legacy Of Magick" series, and has been featured in USA TODAY'S HEA column. Ellen lives an enchanted life in Missouri. Please visit her online at:
www.ellendugan.com
www.facebook.com/ellen.dugan

Made in United States
Troutdale, OR
07/07/2025

32705642R00086